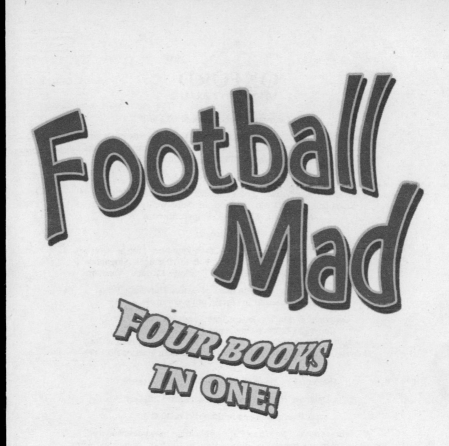

Football Mad

FOUR BOOKS IN ONE!

D0262627

OXFORD
UNIVERSITY PRESS

OXFORD
UNIVERSITY PRESS

Great Clarendon Street, Oxford OX2 6DP

Oxford University Press is a department of the University of Oxford.
It furthers the University's objective of excellence in research, scholarship,
and education by publishing worldwide in

Oxford   New York

Auckland   Cape Town   Dar es Salaam   Hong Kong   Karachi
Kuala Lumpur   Madrid   Melbourne   Mexico City   Nairobi
New Delhi   Shanghai   Taipei   Toronto

With offices in

Argentina   Austria   Brazil   Chile   Czech Republic   France   Greece
Guatemala   Hungary   Italy   Japan   Poland   Portugal   Singapore
South Korea   Switzerland   Thailand   Turkey   Ukraine   Vietnam

Oxford is a registered trade mark of Oxford University Press
in the UK and in certain other countries

British Library Cataloguing in Publication Data

Data available

ISBN 978 0 19 275513 1

5 7 9 10 8 6

Printed in Great Britain by
Cox & Wyman Ltd, Reading, Berkshire

Paper used in the production of this book is a natural,
recyclable product made from wood grown in sustainable forests.
The manufacturing process conforms to the environmental
regulations of the country of origin.

Mark's Dream Team

Alan MacDonald

Illustrated by Clive Goodyer

Contents

The Last Autograph

The trouble with Kenny is that he's got too much imagination. Take football, for instance. Kenny imagines he's a brilliant footballer, he really does. To hear Kenny talk you'd think it's only a matter of time before he gets picked for England. Yet the truth is you wouldn't pick Kenny for your team unless everybody else had died of bubonic plague. It's not that he doesn't try hard, he does, it's just that he lacks basic things—like skill. Kenny's always telling me he's a midfielder, but that's only because he can't score goals and he couldn't tackle a flea. What he does most of the time is to run up and down the pitch, screaming 'Pass! Pass!' to anyone who will listen. And if you do pass, you won't see the ball again because he dribbles around in circles until he loses it.

Don't get me wrong, Kenny is my best friend and I'd stick up for him against anyone. But when it came to picking my team for the tournament I should have told him straight out he wasn't in it. That way I would have saved myself all the trouble that came later.

It all started with Robbie Kidd's autograph. You might think getting an autograph is a daft reason to enter a football tournament but that's why I did it. Robbie Kidd is City's five-million-pound striker and he's my all time favourite player. Last season he scored twenty-one goals for City. Almost every replica City shirt you see round our way has a number nine and the name 'KIDD' on the back. I've got one myself. That's why I was desperate to get his autograph to complete my collection.

I already had the autographs of every other player in City's first team. I got most of them at an open day at the City ground to meet the players; but somehow I never managed to get near Robbie Kidd that day. Whenever I looked there was a vast sea of people milling round him. I queued for ages but, just when I got near the front, Robbie announced he had to go. After that, getting Robbie Kidd's autograph became my personal mission in life. It was almost an obsession with me. In fact Kenny had taken to snoring every time I mentioned the subject.

Not long after, I had the chance to get Robbie Kidd's autograph. Kenny spotted him going into a hairdresser's and, once he'd convinced me he wasn't joking, we followed.

As soon as we walked through the door I knew we'd made a mistake. It was nothing like the barber's where I go to get my hair cut.

Everything about the place said '*expensive*' in big letters. Behind a desk sat a man with a ponytail who was staring at us as if we'd just brought in a nasty smell from the street.

'Can I help you?' he asked.

Kenny looked at me. His face plainly said, 'Run. Let's get out of here.'

But I wanted that autograph badly.

'Um . . . yes . . . ' I said hesitantly. Then, with a sudden inspiration, 'My friend needs a haircut.'

Kenny shot me a look of total horror. 'I don't think I do,' he muttered.

'Yes you *do*, Kenny,' I replied. 'Remember?'

Kenny glared back at me. Well, what else could I have said? My hair's short while Kenny's sticks up all over the place like a loo brush. It was obvious he was the one who needed a haircut.

A moment later we were sitting on one of the enormous sofas. I pretended to read a magazine, while scanning the room for Robbie Kidd.

'What are you playing at?' Kenny whispered furiously.

'Relax. Just playing for time,' I said. 'Look, he's over there.'

I'd spotted Robbie Kidd in the chair furthest from the door. He was leaning his head back over a sink having his hair washed by an assistant.

'Let's get this straight,' hissed Kenny. 'I am NOT having my hair cut.'

'OK, OK.'

'Have you seen the prices?'

I had. They started at twenty pounds and climbed steeply upwards. Twenty pounds—that was two months pocket money!

'As soon as I've got his autograph, we'll go,' I told Kenny.

'How?' he said. 'You told them I'm having my hair cut.'

I shrugged. 'We just say we changed our minds.'

'I'm going to get you for this,' muttered Kenny bitterly.

We waited. At last Robbie Kidd was having his hair dried with a towel. He must have made some joke because the girl drying his hair was laughing.

'Now!' whispered Kenny urgently. 'Get over there.'

But before I could move, a girl with short red hair came over to us.

'I'm Judy,' she said in a bored voice. 'Which one's for the chop then?'

'Pardon?' I said.

'Which of you wants his hair cut?'

I pointed dumbly at Kenny. Without a word he got up and followed Judy over to an empty black chair like a condemned man approaching the firing squad. All the time he kept looking back at me, imploring me to do something. He was about to have the most expensive haircut of his life. I felt in my pockets and quickly counted my change. It came to 75p—which I was saving for my bus fare home. It was all the money I had. Kenny must have had the same thought. As Judy picked up her scissors, he suddenly sprang out of the chair as if he'd been stung by a bee.

'I'm sorry, I've changed my mind,' he blurted out.

'What's the matter?' said Judy. But Kenny

didn't stick around for explanations. Before I could stop him, he'd bolted out of the door, slamming it so hard behind him that I half expected the glass to shatter. Everyone in the room abruptly stopped talking and looked over to see what the commotion was about. As I got awkwardly to my feet, they turned their gaze on me. 'Sorry about that,' I said. 'He's um . . . he's got nits.'

This got a bigger reaction than I'd expected. Several people gasped and recoiled from me in

horror, clearly believing I was crawling with bugs too. The ponytailed assistant flattened himself against the wall to let me get to the door. Out of the corner of my eye I could see Robbie Kidd watching all this and grinning hugely.

'He's having treatment but he gets embarrassed,' I burbled on. 'So, well, thanks anyway for the . . . um . . . '

At last I'd reached the door. I fumbled for the handle, got it open, and stumbled blindly out of the shop.

Outside, Kenny was waiting for me.

'Well? Did you get his autograph?' he asked.

I gave him a withering look. 'Thanks,' I said. 'You were a real help.'

The whole episode was a fiasco. Even now I cringe with embarrassment when I think about it. And it might have been the end of the story; there would have been no Endsley Eagles, no football tournament, and no autograph. But it didn't end there—a few weeks later I saw the report in the newspaper. It had to be Fate, I told myself. Fate stepped in to give me one last chance to get Robbie Kidd's autograph. Of course, at the time I hadn't a clue what I was letting myself in for—otherwise I might have told Fate to mind its own business.

Fate and Chips

I had just ordered five portions of fish and chips when we saw it. It was a Saturday evening and Kenny and I had been sent to the fish and chip shop to get supper for my family. The newspaper was lying open on the counter next to the plastic salt cellar and the vinegar pot. The page had got stains all over it from people's greasy fingers so I didn't take much notice. It was Kenny who spotted the picture. He stabbed a finger at a photograph near the top of the page. 'Look, it's Robbie Kidd.'

It was unmistakably him. What's more, there was an article underneath the photo which was even more interesting. It said:

CITY TO HOST SOCCER TOURNAMENT

Budding soccer stars will get a chance to show their skills next month in an exciting new tournament at the City ground. The competition is open to any five-a-side teams in the under-12 age group. City idol Robbie Kidd will be on hand to present the trophy to the winning side . . .

I didn't need to read any more. I was so excited I almost forgot to pay for our fish and chips. Checking that no one was looking I folded the page with the article and hid it in my pocket. Once we were outside the shop I said, 'Kenny, listen. This is it. This is the answer.' I read the article out loud to him.

'Good idea, we could go along and watch,' he said.

I shook my head. He hadn't grasped it yet. 'This is how I'll meet Robbie Kidd,' I said. 'I'll be standing right next to him.'

'How do you work that out?'

'When he hands me the trophy, thicko. I'm

going to enter a team in that tournament and win.'

Kenny gaped at me as he took this in. Then his face lit up.

'Yeah,' he said. 'We could as well. We could get Martin—he's the best goalie in the whole school. And Rashid—he'd play . . . '

'I'll play up front,' I said.

'And I'll be midfield . . . ' said Kenny.

I stopped in my tracks. 'You?'

'Yeah, of course,' said Kenny. 'Midfield. I always play midfield.' He blinked at me for a moment and adjusted his glasses.

'Right,' I agreed quickly. 'You in midfield and me up front. We're bound to win. We'll be unstoppable.'

All the way home and over supper, Kenny and I talked excitedly about the tournament. We discussed our team colours and what we should call ourselves. But all the time there was a nagging doubt at the back of my mind. It was Kenny. OK, I'm not saying I'm wonder boy myself but I'm good enough to make the subs' bench for our school team. But Kenny? As

I've mentioned he's as much use as a short-sighted penguin. You can imagine how thrilled I felt having him on my team. I wanted to win that tournament more than anything. Robbie Kidd would be there watching and I pictured myself coming away with the trophy under my arm and his autograph in my book. But my plan all depended on winning. If we were knocked out before the final I might never get anywhere near Robbie Kidd. Kenny was the weak link in the whole plan. With him on our side I didn't see us getting past the first round.

That was my mistake. I should have told him there and then. But I just couldn't do it. When I looked at Kenny, I knew how much it would hurt his feelings if I left him out. Besides, he was my best friend and we did everything together. So I said nothing and let him go on believing he'd be in the team. Stupid, I know, but I was only just getting started. You'd be surprised just how stupid I can be.

Kenny and I sat down right away and completed the entry form at the bottom of the newspaper article. We called our team Endsley

Eagles (after Endsley Drive, which is the name of my road.) Kenny wanted to call us Haddock United so that we could get sponsorship from the fish and chip shop, but I said no one would take us seriously with a name like that. Sealing the envelope, I placed it on the table ready to post in the morning.

As I said goodbye to Kenny that evening, he was so excited he could hardly stop talking.

'Wait till they hear this at school,' he kept saying. 'Me! Playing at the City ground. Think of that, eh? My dad will never believe it.'

I watched him cross the road and dribble an imaginary ball along the pavement, before thumping it home between two parked cars. He stood with both arms in the air, head thrown back, taking the applause of the crowd on the empty street. Sometimes I seriously worry about Kenny.

3

Nine into Five

'We're still one player short,' Kenny reminded me as we walked into school on Monday morning. 'Who are we going to ask?'

I'd already given the matter some thought. So far, we'd decided on four players for the Eagles—Martin, Rashid, Kenny, and me. I hadn't asked Martin and Rashid yet but I was pretty sure they'd leap at the chance to play. After all, anyone who turned down a chance of playing at the City ground would need their head examined.

Martin was the obvious choice for goalkeeper. Apart from being the school goalie, he's the best keeper I know. He's not much taller than me but he's fast on his feet and a great shot stopper. Rashid is another of my friends who's in the school team. He plays as a central defender and he's got long legs that he uses to steal the ball away from you just when you think you've got past him. I knew I could rely on Rashid to keep things tight at the back. He didn't go wandering upfield in search of glory like most defenders I know. That left Kenny and me. It would be my job to score the goals and Kenny could—well, Kenny could make a nuisance of himself (probably to both sides).

Martin, Rashid, Kenny, and me—it still left us one player short. I'd run through the team in my head a hundred times and I hadn't yet come up with the fifth player. It wasn't that we were short of choices, I could have asked anyone in the school, but we didn't need just anyone. Whoever we chose had to be good enough to make up for Kenny's shortcomings in midfield. It had to be someone who could tackle hard, run with the ball, and preferably score goals too. (I couldn't do it all by myself.)

As Kenny and I walked into the playground a football hummed through the air, narrowly missing my head. It thumped against the railings and rebounded at my feet.

'Hey, careful!' I said. 'That nearly—'

I stopped in mid sentence. The boy coming to retrieve the ball was Steve Spicer. He eyed me from under his dark fringe of hair.

'Yeah?'

'Nothing,' I said. 'Sorry, I . . . I wasn't looking, Steve.'

Spicer nodded. He flicked the ball up with his foot and caught it neatly. Then he ran back to the game he was playing.

'Sorry, Steve,' mimicked Kenny in a grovelling voice. 'Sorry, did my head get in the way of your ball, Steve?'

I wasn't listening. I was staring after the fifth player we needed for Endsley Eagles. It was amazing that I'd never thought of it before.

'Spicer?' Kenny was incredulous. 'You've got to be joking!'

'Why?' I said. 'He's the best player in the school.'

'Yes, but you know what he's like,' argued Kenny. 'He's a psycho. He should be locked up.'

'Yes,' I agreed. 'But he's also a fantastic footballer.'

'And he's a big head,' Kenny went on. 'He thinks he can boss everyone around.'

'I'm not asking you to like him,' I said. 'We just get him to help us win the tournament.'

'No,' said Kenny flatly. 'He'll spoil everything. Anyway, there are loads of other people we could ask.'

We were interrupted by the bell calling us into school so we didn't finish the argument. Yet the more I thought about it, the more the idea grew on me. Spicer was exactly what we needed.

I was once substitute for a school match where the opposing team had a slight, fair-haired lad who was a good dribbler. His favourite trick was to roll the ball under his foot and dart away before you could tackle him. He tried this trick successfully three or four times in the opening ten minutes of the game. Then he came face to face with Spicer. The two of them stood facing each other—the fair-haired lad with his foot on the ball, Spicer watching him like a wolf eyeing his dinner. The lad rolled the ball under his foot. A second later he was catapulted into the air as Spicer bowled him over with the force of a hurricane and steamed away with the ball. The referee awarded a foul but Spicer had made his point. After that the tricky dribbler hung out on the wing and passed the ball whenever it came his way.

Spicer played football as if he was waging a personal war. There was a furious energy about him. I'd seen him ride three or four tackles on his way into the penalty area, brushing defenders aside like fleas, before thumping the ball venomously into the net. Everyone in our school was scared of him and with good reason. Spicer had a reputation for getting into fights and no one in their right mind wanted to fight him.

Needless to say, Spicer wasn't a friend of ours. Kenny and I instinctively kept well out of his way, which was easy since he wasn't in our class. Yet the more I considered it, the more I thought it made perfect sense. Spicer was the key to us winning the tournament. With him on our side we'd be unbeatable and Robbie Kidd's autograph would be mine for the asking. There was only one question—could I persuade Spicer to play for us?

At break time I spoke to Martin and Rashid who, as I predicted, both eagerly accepted the invitation to play for the Eagles. The prospect of playing at the City ground was enough to make them bug-eyed with excitement.

Martin decided the tournament was just a way of talent spotting youngsters to play for City. 'You wait,' he assured us. 'If we reach the final, they'll sign me up afterwards. There'll be dozens of talent scouts watching, that's the whole point.'

When I mentioned Spicer might be playing for us, they were both astounded.

'Really?' said Rashid. 'How did you get him?'

'Well, I haven't yet,' I said casually. 'But he's bound to say yes. I'm going to have a chat with him later.' Martin and Rashid exchanged looks. 'Having a chat' with Spicer was like saying you were going swimming with sharks.

As it turned out I had the chance to speak to Spicer at lunch time. I spotted him sitting on a table next to Todd Morton, eating his lunch. Todd Morton was a red-haired, freckly boy who played up front for the school team. He hung around Spicer like a pet puppy, wagging his tail whenever Spicer gave him an order.

I approached the table rather nervously, carrying my tray. I still hadn't worked out how I was going to start the conversation.

'Hi,' I said. 'Anyone sitting here?' I indicated the chair opposite Spicer with a nod.

Spicer looked at the empty chair, then at me. 'You trying to be funny?'

'No, no,' I said quickly. 'I just wondered if maybe someone was sitting here and you were saving it for them till they got back—or something.'

I was starting to babble so I sat down quickly and busied myself eating my beefburger and chips. Spicer and Todd Morton carried on finishing their apple crumble as if I wasn't there. Neither of them spoke. Spicer was hunched over his bowl with his arms round it, as if someone might try to steal it from him. (Rumour had it there were three older Spicer brothers at home, each bigger and meaner than he was.) He ate quickly, spooning the pudding into his mouth and slurping noisily. There was a small piece of crumble stuck to his cheek. Before I'd worked out how to open the conversation, he slid his empty bowl across to Todd.

'Right, I'm off. Take that to the hatch for me.' He stood up and pushed his chair back.

Sensing it was now or never, I took a breath. 'Wait,' I said. 'Steve, there's something I wanted to ask you.'

Spicer looked at me as if he'd forgotten I was there. 'Yeah?'

'It's just I'm getting this team together for a tournament.'

'What sort of team? Tiddlywinks?' said Spicer. He glanced at Todd Morton who sniggered on cue.

'A football team,' I said. 'Five-a-side. We're called Endsley Eagles.'

'Big thrills. So what?'

'Well, so I thought maybe you could play for us. I mean you're the best player in the school so . . . '

Spicer interrupted. 'Why should I play for your crummy little team?'

I paused before playing my ace. 'No reason.

It's just the tournament's being held at the City ground. In fact, the trophy's going to be presented by Robbie Kidd.'

'Robbie Kidd?'

Spicer's mouth had dropped open. Suddenly he was sitting down opposite me paying full attention. Todd Morton had sat down too and they were firing questions at me. When is it? they wanted to know. How did I hear about it? Was I absolutely certain that Robbie Kidd was going to be there? I filled them in on all the details.

'Who else is in the team?' asked Spicer when I'd finished.

'Well, obviously we'll have Martin in goal. Then there's Rashid, me, you, and um . . . Kenny.'

'Kenny? Kenny Bird?' said Spicer. 'That gormless idiot? He can't play to save his life.'

'I know he's not in the school team,' I said. 'But he's not that bad.'

'What about me?' Todd Morton suggested. 'I don't mind playing.'

'Yeah, but we've already got a team,' I said.

Spicer shook his head. 'Todd's ten times better than Birdbrain. You want to win this thing, don't you?'

'Yeah,' I said, 'but we already . . . '

'Anyway you need six,' Spicer interrupted.

'Six?'

'Yeah. You can't enter a tournament without a sub. So with me and Todd that makes six. What's your problem?'

Spicer shook his dark fringe out of his eyes and stared me out. He had an unnerving way of holding your gaze and saying nothing, daring you to disagree with him.

'Nothing,' I said after a pause. 'No problem at all. That's settled then. You and Todd, great.'

Getting up from the table, I walked away. It hadn't gone quite the way I'd planned. Todd Morton was a creep and I hadn't bargained on having him in the team. All the same, he was a decent footballer and the main thing was I'd persuaded Spicer to play. With him on our side, I felt we had a real chance of winning the tournament. All in all I reckoned I'd handled the whole thing pretty well. Spicer hadn't even tried to hit me.

I went out to the playground to look for Kenny and the others to tell them the news. But before I could find them I was stopped by two boys from our class—Andy Smart and Ryan James.

'Is it true?' Andy wanted to know.

'Is what true?' I said.

'That you've got a team and you're going to play at the City ground?'

'Who told you that?' I asked.

'Kenny. He's going round telling everyone he's going to meet Robbie Kidd.'

I rolled my eyes. Trust Kenny to have blabbed it all round the school.

'Yes,' I said. 'It's true, what about it?'

'Let me play,' pleaded Andy. 'I could play up front, you've seen me. Or defence even. I don't mind. I'll play anywhere.'

'The thing is . . . ' I began.

Ryan James cut in. 'What about me? I'm miles better than Kenny. He's useless.'

They both started talking at once, telling me why I'd be mad not to pick them. I found myself backing away until I was pressed up against a wall.

'Look!' I said, finally getting a word in edgeways. 'The thing is, I can't pick either of you. We've got all the players we need.'

'That's not what Kenny told us,' replied Andy. 'He said you were still one player short.'

He took something out of his school bag and placed it in my hands. It was his Premiership Sticker Book which I vaguely remembered admiring at his house once. My own sticker collection had been abandoned after a week but Andy had diligently collected and swapped until he had every player in the Premiership.

'What's this?' I asked.

'It's yours. You can keep it,' said Andy.

'Don't be daft. It took you ages to collect all these.'

'Just think about it,' said Andy. 'That's all I'm saying. I'd give anything to play at the City ground. Anything.'

I sighed heavily. 'Look, I can't promise anything . . . '

Andy grinned and slapped me on the back. 'Thanks, Mark. You won't regret it.'

'And me too?' said Ryan. 'I'm miles better than Kenny. You know I am.'

Before I could say any more they'd walked off, both convinced they were a certainty for the team.

I told you before I can be stupid. My trouble is I just can't say no to people. It's when they look at me in that pleading way. Maybe it's because I know what it feels like not to be picked. It's happened to me loads of times for the school team and it's the worst feeling in the world. So when someone asks me—begs me—to let them play, I say nothing. The problem is nothing turns out to be worse than saying no.

By the end of that day I counted up the players I had for Endsley Eagles. Besides me and Kenny there was now Martin, Rashid, Spicer, Todd, Andy, Ryan, and Danny Lawrence. (I haven't mentioned Danny, he followed me around the rest of that day nagging until I finally gave in and promised to give him a chance.) At the start of the day we were a player short, now we had a squad of nine players, all convinced they were in the team. Don't ask me how it happened. Personally I blamed Kenny for opening his big mouth.

On Trial

It was bound to end in disaster. For the next couple of days I went around hoping the whole mess would sort itself out. Maybe some of the team would get cold feet or go down with chickenpox and I'd miraculously find myself back with only five players again. Of course it didn't happen. With the tournament less than a week away, everyone kept telling me how much they were looking forward to playing.

It was Kenny who suggested the training session. After all, he pointed out, we hadn't got much time to get used to playing together as a team. Rashid and Martin were all in favour and in the end I had to agree. We fixed our first training session to be held in the local park after school on Wednesday. When I mentioned that I'd tell Spicer, Kenny gave me a surprised look.

'Spicer? What for? I thought we weren't asking him.'

'No,' I said. 'You didn't want to ask him, Kenny. I did.'

'Well what about Andy? Didn't you speak to him?'

'Andy . . . ?'

'Yes, you promised he'd be in the team. That's what he told me.'

'I didn't promise anyone!' I said, starting to getting flustered.

'Then who is playing, Mark?' asked Rashid.

'Yeah, who's in the team besides us four?' demanded Martin.

'I . . . um . . . let's just see who turns up,' I said and walked away quickly, before they could ask any more questions.

Word about the training session soon got around. The news that Endsley Eagles were going to play in a tournament at the City ground had become the talk of the school. People in my class were treating me with a new

respect and I noticed younger kids pointing me out in the playground to their friends. 'That's Mark Denton. The one who's going to meet Robbie Kidd and get his autograph.' (Kenny had told everyone about my quest to get the last autograph.) I would have enjoyed the attention, if I hadn't been so worried about the training session. The questions kept buzzing round my head. Who was I going to leave out? And, worse still, how was I going to break it to them? If I told Andy, Ryan, or Danny they were out, they'd accuse me of breaking promises. If I dropped Spicer or Todd I might as well dig my own grave and jump in to save them the trouble of killing me. The way I saw it, at least four people were going to end up hating me by the end of the day. I was beginning to wish I'd never started to manage my own football team.

I was late getting to the park, because for a long time I'd sat in my bedroom looking at my autograph book. I stared at the blank page in the book—the one waiting for Robbie Kidd's signature. This was the reason I'd started the Eagles, I reminded myself. The whole point of entering the tournament was to win. If we were knocked out before the final there was no certainty I'd get close enough to Robbie Kidd to ask for his autograph. Managers can't afford to be popular, I thought. You just have to pick your best side and it's tough on whoever is left out.

I arrived at the park resolved that I was going to make some hard decisions. But my heart sank when I saw the others waiting for me by the pitch. They were all there—all nine of them—and the arguments had started already.

Spicer turned on me before I'd even had a chance to say hello.

'What's going on? Who invited this bunch of losers?' he demanded.

'Tell him, Mark,' complained Andy. 'Tell Spicer I'm in the team.'

'Yes, and tell him he can go home and take Freckles with him too,' said Kenny, pointing at Todd.

'Watch it, Birdbrain,' said Spicer, taking a step forward.

Things were getting out of hand. Luckily Rashid stepped between Kenny and Spicer, trying to calm everyone down.

'It's your team, Mark,' he said. 'Just tell us who's playing. Then we can get started.'

Everyone looked at me. And that's when the solution came to me out of the blue. I didn't know why I'd never thought of it before. Nine players was almost enough for *two* five-a-side teams.

'I can explain,' I said. 'We're going to have a trial game.'

'A what?' asked Kenny.

'A trial game. You know, just like a professional club. They watch you play in a match and then they pick the best players from either side.'

'Hang on,' said Kenny. 'I thought this was a training session. We already picked the team, Mark. We agreed on it.' A note of panic was creeping into his voice which I tried to ignore.

'What's up, Speccy?' taunted Spicer. 'Scared you're not good enough?'

'Suits me,' said Todd Morton with a shrug. 'I'll play against anyone.'

Danny Lawrence nodded. 'Why not? A trial's fair to everyone. As long as there's no favouritism, Mark.'

I promised I would be impartial. Only Kenny looked unhappy with the idea. I avoided his gaze as we picked sides with Spicer and myself as captains. I picked Martin, Rashid, Ryan, and Kenny on my side. Spicer picked Todd, Andy, and Danny. The sides weren't even but that didn't seem to bother Spicer unduly. He probably felt he was worth two of us in any case.

We lined up for kick off with Martin in goal, Rashid and Ryan in defence, and Kenny and me up front. 'Pass it around and keep it away from Spicer,' I whispered to Kenny.

Kenny didn't answer, evidently still sulking that he had to go through with this charade. He pushed his glasses up his nose and squared his bony shoulders. As usual he was wearing his one and only football shirt, an old City one that had been washed so many times the blue had faded to a dirty grey.

From kick-off I passed the ball to Kenny who knocked it back to Rashid. Rashid brought the ball forward and slipped it out to me on the wing. Andy slid in to tackle me but I side-stepped him and spotted Kenny in space near the goal. 'Kenny!' I shouted and sent him a perfect pass. Normally I would have tried to score myself, but I was still feeling guilty. I wanted to give Kenny every chance to prove he was worth his place in the team.

Kenny collected the ball with his back to goal and turned to try and shoot. Unfortunately he'd forgotten completely about Spicer. At the last moment, he tried to jump out of the way, but it was too late. The crunch of the tackle could be heard all over the park.

'Yeeearggh!' howled Kenny and collapsed to the ground, holding his leg.

Spicer moved away with the ball, without even a backward glance. In a few strides he was past me and bearing down on our goal. To his credit,

Rashid tried to tackle him, but Spicer surged past him as if he wasn't there. He struck his shot hard and low towards the corner. It looked like a certain goal until Martin dived full length and got his fingertips to it, turning it round the pile of coats we were using for goal posts.

'Great save, Martin!' I shouted. Spicer shook his head, furious with himself for not scoring. He collected the ball to take the corner himself while I ran back to help Rashid and Ryan defend. Looking upfield, I could see Kenny still limping around, rubbing his leg and looking aggrieved. Spicer hit an inswinging corner aimed towards the near post. I stepped forward to head it away but Todd Morton suddenly appeared in front of me and glanced the ball into the empty goal.

'We practised that one for the school team,' he gloated. 'Works every time.'

'Come on, Kenny,' I said under my breath as we lined up to take the kick off. 'They're making us look stupid.'

Kenny was still seething about Spicer's tackle on him. 'He's an animal,' he muttered. 'They should put him in the zoo.'

Things didn't get any better. The game continued to be one-way traffic, even though we were the side with the extra player. In our defence Ryan was scared stiff of Spicer, which left Rashid to try and hold out on his own. Time and again, Martin had to pull off a great save to keep us in the game. Even so, it wasn't long before the score crept up to 5–0. Todd scored twice while Spicer helped himself to a hat trick. I managed to pull one goal back with a long shot that Danny fumbled in goal, but that was the only reply we managed.

Kenny had been little more than a spectator since Spicer had flattened him. He limped around upfield and occasionally called for a pass without much conviction. Then, right near the end of the game, he was gifted the best chance of the game. Rashid broke up an attack and swept the ball upfield to find Kenny unmarked and with a clear run on goal. By the time Spicer was hot on his heels, Kenny was into the penalty area and looked certain to score.

'Shoot, Kenny! Shoot!' I shouted, seeing Spicer gathering himself for a sliding tackle.

Maybe it was the fear of another one of Spicer's crunching tackles that put him off. Or maybe it was knowing that everyone expected him to score. Whatever the reason, the pressure was too much. Kenny sliced the ball off the outside of his boot and watched it miss the goal by a mile. The ball struck a low branch of a tree and sent a flock of startled sparrows twittering into the sky.

Some of the others hooted with laughter. 'Nice shooting, Birdbrain!' said Spicer, patting Kenny on the head.

I called a halt to the game soon after that. I'd seen more than enough.

The others gathered round me, panting to catch their breath.

'Well?' said Spicer. 'Let's hear it then, captain. Tell us the team.'

5

Fall Out

They were all looking at me expectantly and I knew the decision couldn't be put off any longer. It was better to get it over with.

'OK,' I said, trying not to look anyone in the eye. 'I can't pick everyone, so here it is. In goal Martin. Rashid in defence. Midfield—me and Steve,' I said, nodding at Spicer. 'Up front . . . ' I paused. 'Up front we'll play Todd.'

There was a groan from Andy, Ryan, and Danny. They shook their heads in disbelief. That didn't bother me so much as Kenny. He was standing pale and tight-lipped at the back of the group. He hadn't spoken a word but he was staring at me resentfully.

'Kenny, I'd like you to be sub . . . ' I began.

'You can stick it,' he said, his voice thick and harsh.

'Come on, Kenny . . . '

'No! Stuff that!' He was shaking with anger now. 'I don't want to be sub for your poxy team, Mark.'

He turned to walk away, but swung round again after only a few steps.

'You want to know something?' he said. 'There wouldn't be an Endsley Eagles if it wasn't for me. I was the one who saw the report in the paper. I helped to think of the name. It was us who started this team, Mark, remember? You and me. And now you've got the nerve to say I can be sub, like you're doing me a big favour. Well, thanks, thanks a lot, but you can stick it.'

Kenny stalked off towards the park gate, his socks rolled down to his pale thin ankles. I had a strong urge to run after him and grab him by the arm. To say it was all a joke, that he was right, that the Eagles were as much his team as mine, but it was way too late for that.

Spicer watched him go with a thin smile. 'Ahh, poor baby,' he said. 'Let him go crying to his mum.'

The next morning, Kenny didn't call for me on the way to school. Most days he drops in about quarter to nine and we walk the last part of the journey together. But on Thursday I waited until ten to nine and there was no ring at the door bell.

I didn't blame him for still being mad at me. I knew how much it meant to him playing at the City ground. He'd told everyone at school about it, and now the word would go round that he'd been dropped from the team. It was humiliating and it was all my fault. But, put yourself in my shoes, what else could I have done? How could I pick Kenny after the way he played in that trial game? It would have been obvious to everyone that I was just choosing my best friend. Even Kenny's own mother wouldn't have picked him after that open goal he missed. I had to leave him out to be fair to the others. And besides, there was another reason—I wanted to win the tournament and I wanted Robbie Kidd's autograph. If I was honest it was a relief that I had an excuse to drop Kenny.

All the same, don't get the idea I felt good about it. And I didn't feel any better when I got to school. There was Kenny standing in the playground with Andy Smart and Ryan James. As I walked by they all turned and looked at me as if I'd crawled out from under a stone.

'Got my sticker book?' demanded Andy.

I pulled it out of my school bag and handed it over. I'd never asked for it in the first place so I didn't know why he was acting all high and mighty.

Kenny didn't say anything, didn't even give a nod in my direction. He went back to telling Andy and Ryan about some goofy programme he'd been watching on TV the night before. I walked off and left the three of them to it. It felt strange standing on my own in the playground, hoping that the bell would go soon.

The rest of the day it was the same story.

Kenny hung around with his new buddies, Andy and Ryan, and avoided me like the plague. He even moved tables in class so that he wouldn't have to sit next to me.

At afternoon break I went looking for Martin and Rashid and caught up with them in the playground.

'It's OK,' said Martin when he saw me. 'We already know.'

'Know what?' I asked mystified.

'About training tonight. Didn't Spicer talk to you about it?'

'No,' I said, 'I haven't seen him all day.'

'Oh.' Martin looked a little uncomfortable.

'Anyway,' said Rashid, 'we're meeting at four at the old scout hut. Spicer reckons we need to practise five-a-side rules and the scout hut's better than the park.'

'The goals are just the right size,' enthused Martin.

'Just hold on,' I said. 'How come no one's asked me about this?'

Neither of them answered.

'I thought I was captain of this team?'

''Course you are, Mark,' said Rashid.

'Then how come Spicer is fixing training sessions and telling you all what to do?'

Martin looked at the ground, sullenly. 'It's not our fault. Talk to Spicer,' he said.

I couldn't find Spicer before the end of break and there was no sign of him at the end of school either. I decided the only thing I could do was turn up at the scout hut like everyone else and try to straighten things out with him. I couldn't help feeling annoyed. I was the one who'd invited Spicer to play for the Eagles in the first place and now he was acting as if it was his team. It was stupid, I know, but I even started to wonder if he'd planned to tell me about the training session. It seemed as if Spicer had made sure to inform everyone except me. What was going on?

6

Votes for Captain

At four o'clock, I made my way along the overgrown path to the meeting place. The old scout hut was a shabby building at the end of Church Road. In fact, it hadn't been used as a scout hut for years but the name had stuck. Nettles grew around the entrance and there was a rusty padlock on the door. In any case we were more interested in what lay round the back. Following the path through a wilderness of trees and bushes, you eventually came to some steps which led down unexpectedly to an ancient tennis court. The net had disappeared long ago, leaving only the faint outline of the court on the cracked surface. It made a perfect five-a-side pitch which someone had recognized by painting the outline of goal posts at either end on the wooden boards that skirted the wire fencing.

As I reached the path, I could hear voices coming from the court at the back. The others had evidently arrived before me. Below me I could hear one voice louder and more insistent than the others. It was unmistakably Spicer's and something made me hang back behind the corner of the scout hut to listen.

'The captain's always the best player,' he was saying. 'You look at any professional team.'

'Yeah, Steve, but it's not your team. It's Mark's. He started it.' The second voice was Rashid's.

'So what?' said Spicer. 'Any idiot can fill in a form. I could have done it.'

'But you didn't. Endsley Eagles was Mark's idea.'

Spicer tried a different tack. 'OK, fine, don't say I didn't warn you. If you want to get knocked out first round it's up to you.'

'You don't think we stand a chance?' asked Martin, worriedly.

'Not with a loser like Mark Denton as captain.'

Another voice joined in, Todd Morton's. 'Steve should be captain. It's obvious. He's worth ten of Denton.'

It was fast dawning on me why Spicer hadn't told me about this 'training session'. With me out of the way he was trying to bully the others into making him captain. I couldn't believe his nerve.

'Tell 'em, Steve,' Todd was saying. 'Tell 'em what we talked about earlier.'

Spicer ignored him. 'The point is, everyone here plays for the school team, right? Me, Todd, Martin, and you Rashid. There's only player who isn't good enough.'

'Mark's played for the school team,' protested Rashid.

'Only when we're desperate,' sneered Spicer. 'He never gets a full game. And he reckons he's a striker but let's face it, when did he last score a goal?'

Nobody answered. It was a sore point with me that I'd never scored for the school team.

It's not easy to score when you're only allowed on as sub for the last ten minutes.

Spicer went on, hammering home his argument. 'Think about it. You'll never get another chance like this. Do you want to lose just because of one player?'

'Steve's right,' bleated Todd.

'Ask yourself why is Denton in the team? I'll tell you. Because he picked it, that's why.'

'He's a passenger,' agreed Todd.

'Wait a minute!' Rashid protested. 'Are you saying we kick Mark out? Out of his own team?'

'It's not his team any more,' said Spicer coolly. 'If I'm captain, I pick the side. And I say he's not good enough.'

Something snapped in me when I heard that. All the time I'd been listening to Spicer I was getting more wound up and now I felt I'd explode if I heard another word. In seconds I was bounding down the steps and on to the court. Every face turned towards me in surprise and, for once, even Spicer looked taken aback. He obviously hadn't expected to see me and now he was wondering how much I'd overheard.

'Mark. We were just waiting for you,' he said, forcing a smile.

'Oh were you?' I said. 'Funny, because from what I just heard, you can't wait to get rid of me.' My heart was thumping in my chest and I was breathing hard.

'We weren't in on this, Mark,' Rashid said quietly. 'This was all Spicer's idea.'

I turned back to Spicer, who stood his ground, glaring defiantly.

'Well, it's true, I should be captain. I'm the only decent player in this crummy team and you know it.'

'Well, besides me,' said Todd.

'Shut up!' ordered Spicer. He took a step

forward so that I could feel his warm breath on my face. 'What are you going to do, Markie boy, fight me for it? Go ahead.'

By now I was so enraged, I was ready to throw myself on top of Spicer and take my chances. All that stopped me was knowing that a fight was exactly what Spicer wanted. If he could reduce it to a slugging contest, I knew there'd be only one winner, and it wouldn't be me. Instead I took a step back. 'OK. Fair's fair. There are five of us here. Let's take a vote on it. Who wants Spicer as captain?'

Todd's hand went up immediately. Spicer raised his own hand in the air and glowered at Martin and Rashid. Martin shifted uneasily, but neither of them made a move.

'Who votes I stay as captain?' I asked. My own hand went up and was joined by Rashid's. For a moment I thought my plan might backfire. Martin was hesitating, caught between loyalty to me and fear of what Spicer might do to him. At last, slowly, he raised his hand in the air.

'That settles it then,' I said. 'Three votes to

two. I'm still captain and since I pick the side, I'm dropping you, Spicer. You're off the team.'

'You what?' croaked Spicer in disbelief.

'You heard. We don't need you. Get lost.'

Spicer gave a hollow laugh. 'You're rubbish without me. I'm the only decent player you've got.'

'Not any more.' I said. 'And you can take your freckle-faced poodle with you. We won't be needing him either.'

Spicer narrowed his eyes and bared his yellow teeth. For a moment I thought he was going to lunge at me and pin me to the ground. Then he turned on his heel and stalked off up the steps, with Todd scampering after him. 'You wait, Denton,' he spat back over his shoulder. 'You'll be sorry for this.'

We waited in silence until he'd disappeared, then Rashid burst out laughing.

'Blimey! You were taking a chance, Mark. I thought he was going to murder you!'

'So did I,' I said. I realized my hands were still shaking and hid them in my pockets. 'Anyway. We're better off without those two creeps.'

'Yeah,' said Martin. 'But before you get too pleased with yourself, aren't you forgetting something?'

'What?'

'How are we going to win the tournament with only three players?'

7

Kenny

'Oh, it's you,' said Kenny sourly. 'I thought you'd be out training for the big day. If you want me to come and cheer you on, you're wasting your time.'

It was Friday afternoon—just one week before the tournament—and I was standing at Kenny's front door. I came straight to the point.

'We need you back on the team, Kenny.'

'Yeah sure. As sub,' he said.

'No, in the team. Midfield dynamo. What do you say?'

Kenny's eyes lit up for a second. Then he remembered the way I'd treated him and the blank look returned. He wasn't going to let me off the hook that easily.

'What's made you change your mind?' he asked. 'I thought I wasn't good enough for you.'

Briefly I explained to him what had happened last night at the scout hut.

'Huh,' grunted Kenny with satisfaction. 'Told you, didn't I? I told you Spicer would try to take over.'

'I know,' I admitted. 'I should have listened.'

'So the truth is you only want me back because you can't get a team?'

'Come on, Kenny,' I said. 'There are hundreds of other people we could ask.'

'Great. Why don't you then?'

I sighed. This was proving harder than I'd expected. 'Look, I'm sorry, OK, Kenny? I just got carried away with the idea of winning. I made a mistake and I'm sorry. What else do you want me to say?'

Kenny looked away. 'You could say you think I'm good enough.'

So that's what was eating him. 'Kenny,' I said, 'you're worth ten of Spicer any day.'

His face finally broke into a grin. 'Yeah

right,' he said. 'I'll remind you of that next time I miss an open goal.'

'So does that mean you'll play?'

'Are you kidding? Think I'm gonna miss the chance to play at the City ground? Anyway, I want to be there to make sure Robbie Kidd signs your autograph book. Then I won't have to listen to you droning on about it for another year.'

Kenny was off then, talking tactics and outlining how he thought we should approach our first game. I couldn't help smiling as we walked down to the park to meet the others. The great thing about Kenny is he can't hold a grudge for long. I guessed that the past few days had been as much of a torture to him as they were to me. OK, Kenny may not be the greatest footballer in the world, but I realized I felt better having my best friend back on the team. Kenny is a born optimist and there wasn't a flicker of doubt in his mind that we could win the tournament—Spicer or no Spicer.

'After all,' he reasoned. 'It's like the FA Cup. Anything can happen in a knock-out tournament. We've only got to win a few games and suddenly we're in the final.'

In the week that followed we trained harder than we'd ever done in our lives. Andy Smart didn't need much persuasion to rejoin the team and we discovered that when we tried him in defence he was a natural. I couldn't understand why he'd been trying to play as a striker all this time. Andy's built like a miniature tank and he hasn't got the speed to play up front. Put him in defence alongside Rashid, however, and he was as steady as a rock.

There was one thing we still needed—a coach. Over breakfast on Saturday morning I happened to mention to my dad that we were having trouble with our free kick routines. Dad used to be a referee in amateur football and he took the bait, just as I'd hoped. Soon he was down at the park with us every evening, helping us prepare for the tournament. He had us playing two-touch football so that we learned to move the ball quickly from one player to another. We spent hours crossing the ball and shooting first time, aiming low for the corners the way he taught us. Even Kenny started to gain in confidence in front of goal and was less of a danger to passing seagulls.

Finally we worked on a free kick routine where I pretended I was going hit the ball but at the last moment rolled it to one side for Rashid to shoot. Seven or eight times out of ten it worked with the ball ending up in the net, even though Martin in goal knew what was coming.

At last, the night before the tournament, Dad said we were ready. 'It's up to you now,' he told us. 'You've put in all the hard work, now you've got to make it count on the day. There'll be other good teams, but don't worry about them. You just go out and play the way we've been practising.'

Friday night finally arrived and we piled into two cars and drove to the City ground. The sight of the stadium towering over us made my stomach lurch. I'd been to the ground dozens of times before but that was to watch City play. This time it would be us out there on the pitch. The car park was packed with cars and minibuses, while groups of boys stood around in their kit, shivering in the cold wind.

'Blimey!' I said. 'How many people do you think are here?'

'Probably more than City get for a home game,' laughed my dad. 'At least we might see some decent football tonight.'

'I wonder if that's Robbie Kidd's car,' said Kenny as we parked near a gleaming silver Jaguar. 'I hope you've got your autograph book, Mark.'

For the hundredth time that evening I

checked in the pocket of my sports bag. The autograph book was safe inside. Even if we didn't win the tournament, I tried to tell myself, I'd be happy if I went home with Robbie's signature on the blank page in my book. I wondered if he would be there from the start to watch any of our matches. The thought only made me more nervous. What if we froze when we got out on the pitch and were trounced in the very first round? I tried to put such worries out of my mind, as my dad went in search of a club steward. We were eventually directed towards a large grey building resembling an aircraft hanger. Inside, to our surprise and disappointment, we found ourselves looking at an indoor football pitch.

'Is this where we're playing?' grumbled Kenny. 'I thought we'd be on the actual turf.'

'Don't be daft,' said Rashid. 'They're not going to let a load of kids ruin the pitch, are they?'

'This is better anyway,' said my dad. 'It's a proper five-a-side pitch, you can play the ball off the walls.' He started to point out where we weren't allowed inside the goalkeeper's area but he was interrupted by Kenny.

'Look over there! What's he doing here?'

Standing with a team I'd never seen before was Spicer. He was kitted out like the rest of them in a smart all white strip with a silver star emblazoned on the chest. Our team looked shabby in comparison, in our motley collection of replica City shirts from various seasons. As we were staring, Spicer happened to look our way and came striding over, wearing a smug look on his face.

'So, managed to scrape a team together, did you?'

'Who's that lot you're with?' I asked.

'Astley All Stars,' said Spicer. 'My mate Jason is captain. When they heard I was free, they practically begged me to play for them.'

'That desperate, were they?' said Kenny.

Spicer regarded him icily. 'I hope you're wearing your shin pads, Speccy,' he said. 'You'll need them if I come near you.'

'Well, thanks for coming over,' I said. 'Your mates will be worried about you.'

Spicer gave us a parting smile. 'Try not to get knocked out too early,' he said. 'I'm looking forward to playing you lot.' He jogged back to join his team on the other side of the hall.

Rashid appeared at my shoulder. 'I know that team,' he said. 'I've played against them in the Sunday league.'

'Any good?' I asked.

'Top of the table. It makes you sick, they could probably win this without Spicer.'

I told Rashid it was probably better to keep this information to himself. The rest of our team looked nervous enough without adding to their worries. Kenny was fiddling with his glasses while Andy disappeared to the toilet every five minutes. Neither of them had played in a real match before, let alone in front of a crowd this big. I looked around, hoping to catch a glimpse of Robbie Kidd. There were a number of City's training staff, recognizable by their club tracksuits, but no sign of the star attraction.

The draw for the tournament was displayed on a board behind one goal. There were sixteen teams entered which, according to my calculations meant that we had to win three games if we wanted to reach the final. It didn't sound much—three games, but I had no idea what we were up against. Our first round game was against a team called Cosby Kites. However, when our name was called and we ran out on the pitch, the other team didn't appear. We waited around for five minutes taking practice shots at Martin, but no one could find any trace of the Kites.

'Maybe they've flown off,' suggested Kenny.

Eventually the referee informed us we'd been given a bye into the second round.

'What's a buy?' Andy wanted to know. 'Do we have to pay?'

'No, you big dope,' said Rashid. 'It means we go through.'

'Well, that's great,' said Kenny. 'We're in the second round without having kicked a ball.'

I wasn't so sure. All the waiting around only made me more anxious. Personally I'd rather have got a game under our belts to help settle our nerves. We watched as Spicer's team, the

All Stars, played their first round game and won it without breaking sweat, 5–0.

Andy shook his head when the game was over. 'I hope we don't get drawn against them. It'll be a massacre.'

Finally, our second round match came round, against a team called Parkside Rangers. It took us most of the first half to get into the game. At first we were so nervous, we kept making stupid mistakes and giving the ball away. Then, just before half-time, Rashid took a snap shot from a distance and the goalie almost fumbled it, grabbing it at the second attempt. That gave us confidence and we started to string some passes together. 'Shoot on sight,' I told the others at half-time. 'Aim low for the corners like we practised. The goalie looks dodgy to me.' The plan worked. We won the game 2–1, with goals from Andy and me, though mine was a soft shot the goalkeeper let under his body.

It didn't matter to us, when the whistle went for full-time we were delirious. Kenny went round slapping everyone on the back as if we'd just won the tournament.

'Well done,' my dad said, as we trooped off. 'You can take confidence from that second half. You were starting to play as a team. But they won't all be as easy as that. You've got the semi-final next, so you'll have to improve.'

Again we watched Spicer's All Stars stroll through their match, winning 4–1 with Spicer claiming a hat trick. Mercifully we weren't drawn against them in the semi-final but against a team called Tornadoes. They played in an all red strip and they came on to the pitch like they meant business.

'Look at the size of that number three,' Kenny whispered to me. 'You sure these are all under twelve?'

'Size doesn't mean anything,' I said. 'They're probably all fat and slow.'

The Tornadoes turned out to be far from slow, but they didn't mind using their weight. Several times I was elbowed off the ball by the beefy number three I was up against. At half-time there was nothing between us with the

score at 0–0. Martin had kept us in the game with a great one-handed save while at the other end Kenny had fluffed our only chance.

The second half was much the same, with chances going begging at either end. Then, with a few minutes left, we got a free kick, just outside the goalkeeper's area. It was perfect for what we'd practised in training. The Tornadoes made a three man wall in front of their goal area. I placed the ball and took a long run up as if I was going to try and blast it right through them. At the last moment I checked and rolled the ball to my right where Rashid had ghosted up unnoticed. He struck his shot with the outside of his boot and saw it swerve past the unsighted goalkeeper and into the net.

One–nil. The whistle went soon afterwards and I almost collapsed with relief and exhaustion.

'Well done, lads! Brilliant!' said my dad, putting his arm round me.

'We did it!' Kenny shouted. 'I can't believe it. We did it! We're in the final.'

'Yeah,' said Rashid. 'And guess who we'll be playing.'

He was pointing behind us. We turned to see Steve Spicer gloating across at us. Astley All Stars had still to play their semi-final, but it would take a miracle to stop them reaching the final. That meant if we wanted to win the trophy we'd have to beat

them. Spicer mouthed something that I couldn't make out, then drew a finger across his throat in a gesture we all understood. They were going to murder us.

Final Chance

'Listen,' I said. 'We've got this far. What's to stop us going out and winning this?'

'Are you blind?' said Andy. 'You saw them, Mark. We'll get creamed.'

'Not if we play like we did in the semi,' I argued.

'Let's just try and keep the score down,' said Martin dejectedly. 'I don't want to be picking the ball out of the net six or seven times.'

I shook my head in exasperation. 'You're all talking as if we've lost before we've started. You didn't think we'd get to the final, but we did it. Why can't we win one more game?'

'Because we're playing Astley All Stars,' answered Rashid gloomily.

Before I could reply, Kenny interrupted. 'Listen to yourselves!' he said, angrily. 'It's only Spicer and his smarmy mates we're playing, not Real Madrid!'

'Come on, Kenny, he's the best player in the school,' said Martin.

Kenny rounded on him. 'So what? Why are you all scared of him? He thinks we're just a bunch of losers. Well, let's go out there and show him. Let's wipe that grin off his big ugly face.'

It wasn't the best team talk I'd ever heard but it struck a nerve. We all hated Spicer. We hadn't forgotten the way he'd tried to bully us into making him captain. Nothing could be more satisfying than beating him in the final. And in any case, what had we got to lose by trying? At least we'd have the satisfaction of showing Spicer we could put up a fight.

Out of the corner of my eye I could see the referee checking his watch. I began to talk fast.

'This is how we're going to play it,' I said. 'I'm going to drop back to help Rashid and Andy. We'll have a three man defence and we won't let them past. If one of us gets beaten someone else gets back to cover, right?'

'But who's playing striker?' said Andy.

I turned to Kenny. 'That'll be up to you,' I said. 'Chase everything and don't give them any time on the ball. We've got to frustrate them, put them off their game. Then we hit them on the counter attack and Kenny grabs the winner with one of his thunderbolts.'

Everyone laughed. It was hard to imagine a Kenny thunderbolt. So far the only shot he'd managed was so feeble the goalkeeper could have kept it out with a feather duster.

We ran out on to the pitch for the final. Looking over to the presentation table I saw a figure in a leather jacket emerge through the crowd and shake hands with someone. Robbie

Kidd had arrived just in time for the final. Trust him, I thought, to make his entrance at the last minute. There wasn't time for me to go over and ask for his autograph now. Besides I was too keyed up for the final. I'd have to wait until after the game and hope that the runners up would also be presented with medals. Despite what I'd said to the others I thought the best we could hope for was to keep the scoreline respectable.

As captain I went forward for the toss of the coin to choose ends. The All Stars captain was Spicer's friend Jason. He paused to juggle a ball on his knee and volley it off the pitch. Then he grinned at me, revealing a mouthful of fillings. 'Steve says you lot are so rubbish he walked out on you.'

'Yeah?' I replied. 'Well, he would say that. Nobody likes being dropped, do they?'

Jason's smile faded rapidly; he couldn't tell whether I was joking or not. Round one to the Eagles, I thought, and followed up by winning the toss.

That looked like the only thing we would win. From the kick off the All Stars poured forward and laid siege to our goal. In the first minute Martin had to beat out a stinging shot with his hands, just managing to grab the ball before it bounced out of the area where white shirts were waiting ready to pounce.

'Don't give them space to shoot,' I urged the others. 'Close them down quickly.'

Rashid, Andy, and I spread ourselves in a cordon in front of our goal area. The All Stars seemed puzzled by our reluctance to come out of our own half and attack them. Kenny meanwhile chased the ball from one white shirt to the next like an excited terrier.

'Somebody get rid of this nut,' complained Jason. 'He's making me dizzy.'

Gradually our tactics began to work and impatience crept into the opposition's game. Although they had most of the ball, the All Stars were finding it hard to pierce our three man defence. Rashid in particular was timing his tackles beautifully and bringing the ball away with his long easy stride.

Inevitably it was Spicer who decided enough was enough. As I tried to tackle him,

he pushed the ball past me and sent me sprawling with a shove in the back. Rashid came over to cover but not in time, as Spicer unleashed an unstoppable shot that flew past Martin and crashed against the cross bar making the whole goal shudder. Martin grabbed the ball as it bounced out, but too late, the referee had signalled the ball had crossed the line. Spicer turned away with a look of grim satisfaction and jogged back to the halfway line.

We were grateful to hear the half-time whistle with the score at 1–0.

As we trooped off with our heads down, Spicer brushed past me. 'You wait,' he said.

'We're going to bury you second half. Watch me show you how it's done.'

We stood in a semi-circle, hands on hips and breathing hard.

'It was never over the line,' Martin moaned. 'I saved it. The referee needs Kenny's glasses.'

'Typical,' said Rashid bitterly. 'Just when we were holding out really well.'

'It's not over yet,' I urged. 'All we need is one goal and we're back in it. We'll just have to take a few risks and try to go on the attack.'

As the second half started the All Stars drove forward again, confident that the game was there for the taking. It was just a matter of how many goals they were going to score. Rashid, Andy, and I were forced to defend desperately. But now I started to notice the white shirts weren't passing the ball so smoothly. They were so eager to get their names on the score sheet that they got selfish and held on to the ball too long. This made it easier for us to break up their attacks and it wasn't long before we launched one of our own. With the All Stars backtracking furiously Rashid put me through with only Jason barring my way on the edge of the goalkeeper's area. As he advanced, I prodded the ball through his long legs. I knew I'd pushed it too far into the area, but Jason wasn't taking any chances. Before he could stop himself he'd snaked out a leg to slide the ball back to his keeper. The referee blew a shrill blast on his whistle and pointed to the spot.

'Penalty,' he said. 'The ball was inside the area.'

'Yesss!' I shouted, punching the air. But my joy was cut short when I realized we hadn't chosen anyone to take penalties.

'You take it,' I said to Rashid. 'You're good under pressure.'

'No fear,' said Rashid. 'You take it, you're the captain.'

No one else in the team wanted the responsibility. As I placed the ball on the spot, I couldn't help looking over towards the trophy table. Robbie Kidd was watching me, leaning forward on the barrier so as not to miss anything.

Robbie Kidd is watching me take a penalty! I thought to myself. It was like a dream or maybe a nightmare, I couldn't decide which. I'd seen Robbie take penalties for City. He always tucked them away in the bottom corner, making it look impossibly easy.

'Just imagine you're him,' I told myself. 'Hard and low. Bottom corner. You can do this.'

I took a deep breath, ran up, and struck the ball low to the keeper's right. He guessed correctly and dived full length, one arm outstretched. For an agonizing second I thought he was going to push the ball away but then the net shivered and I realized the ball was in. I'd done it! We'd equalized.

And now the amazing thing happened. All round the arena there was the deafening sound of applause and cheering. Maybe two hundred people or more had stayed to watch the final and it dawned on me that nearly all of them were rooting for us. We were the underdogs and everyone wanted to see us beat the swaggering All Stars. Even Robbie Kidd was grinning and clapping his hands. 1–1 with five minutes to go and now our opponents realized that they had a game on their hands.

As we lined up for kick-off I could see a new determination on the faces of my team mates. The goal had lifted us and with the crowd right behind us, we suddenly felt we might have a chance. However the same 'thought had obviously occurred to our opponents and they pressed forward, eager to re-establish their superiority. Several times Rashid or I had to make a last ditch tackle to prevent the winning goal. With two minutes left Jason got past me and blasted a shot from the edge of the area. It was moving so fast I was sure Martin was beaten until he flung himself down to his right and somehow came up with the ball in his hands. With the white shirts all committed to attack, Martin bowled the ball upfield and found Kenny on his own, near the halfway line.

'Go, Kenny!' I shouted. 'Take it on your own!'

With a look of blind panic, Kenny turned and set off dribbling towards the other end. Someone flashed past me and I realized with a sinking heart who it was. Spicer was lightning fast and he was already homing in on Kenny like a guided missile.

I was too far behind to help Kenny, I could only watch and pray that he'd have the sense to shoot before it was too late. If felt as if the whole crowd was holding its breath, watching the gap close between the dark shadow of Spicer and the ungainly kid with the specs. Inevitably Kenny looked back at the last minute and saw him coming. I knew what came next, I'd seen this moment before: Kenny would blaze the ball high and wide into the crowd and hang his head in despair. But, just as he drew his foot back to shoot, Spicer lunged across him in a desperate tackle. What happened next seemed to take place in slow motion. I saw the goalkeeper dive to his left to stop Kenny's shot. But instead the ball ricocheted off Spicer's foot and looped high in the air. With the keeper struggling to change direction, the ball floated in a gentle arc dropping down under the bar to nestle in the back of the net.

The crowd erupted in wild cheering. We all ran and mobbed Kenny who was standing, open mouthed, doing a passable impression of a goldfish.

'You did it, Kenny!' I shouted above the noise. 'You scored!'

'Yeah I did,' he said proudly, readjusting his glasses. 'Did you see how I sent the keeper the wrong way?'

Spicer was still slumped on the ground, his head in his hands. He was surrounded by teammates who were blaming him for putting through his own goal. I couldn't resist patting him on the shoulder as I went past. 'Nice one, Spicer,' I said. 'You really showed us how it's done.'

There was only a minute for us to play out before the referee blew the full time whistle. The All Stars shook their heads in disbelief. They'd been beaten by two goals in the last five minutes when they'd expected to win by a rugby score. Meanwhile we stood on the pitch drinking in the applause, hardly able to believe that we'd won the final.

All too quickly it was time for the presentation and the moment I'd imagined for so long. In a dream I approached the table where Robbie Kidd stood, waiting to hand me the silver trophy, hung with ribbons in City's blue colours.

'Go on, captain,' murmured Kenny behind me. 'This is what you've been waiting for. Ask him for the autograph.'

And that's when I realized that in all the euphoria of winning the game and doing a lap of honour, I'd forgotten the most important thing I had to do.

'I haven't got it,' I said hoarsely.

'What do you mean?' asked Kenny.

'My autograph book. I left it in the pocket of my bag.'

'You big idiot! Run back and get it.'

There wasn't time. I looked for my dad in the crowd and tried to signal frantically to him to bring my bag. He didn't understand and only grinned like a madman, giving me a big thumbs up sign. And, before I could do anything else, we were being ushered forward for the presentation. Robbie Kidd loomed into view and I felt his large, warm hand shaking mine.

'Well done, lads,' he said. 'That was a great come-back.'

I opened my mouth to say something but no words came out. I seemed to have frozen. The next moment a large silver cup was thrust into my hands and somebody had hung a medal round my neck. It should have been the proudest moment of my life, but all I could think was: *I didn't get his autograph. We came*

*all this way and won the cup and I didn't even
ask him. How stupid can you get?*

I moved forward to let Kenny get his medal
and that's when I heard Robbie Kidd say, 'I *knew*
I'd seen you two before. In the hairdresser's,
right? The boy with the nits.'

Turning round I saw Robbie was shaking
Kenny's hand and laughing.

Kenny had turned crimson. 'I haven't
actually got nits,' he muttered. 'Mark made that

up. You see I had to run out because I couldn't afford the haircut.'

'I'm not surprised,' said Robbie Kidd. 'Twenty quid is daylight robbery.' The whole presentation ceremony had come to a standstill while he stood there chatting to the two of us. 'So if you didn't want a hair cut, what were you doing in a hairdresser's?' he asked.

Kenny looked at me. 'Tell him, Mark.'

'I just wanted your autograph,' I said. 'I've been trying to get it for ages. You see I've got this autograph book and I've got everyone else's but not yours. In fact, that's the whole reason we entered this tournament.'

Robbie Kidd looked at me as if it was the best joke he'd ever heard.

'So where is this famous autograph book then?' he laughed.

'It's in my bag over there. Shall I go and get it?'

'Don't worry,' said Robbie. 'I've got a better idea.'

Still smiling to himself, he took out something from his pocket and signed it with a pen. Then he thrust the folded piece of paper into my hand.

'There you are. Don't lose it. You earned that.'

I walked off in a daze, clutching the silver cup in one hand and Robbie Kidd's autograph in the other.

'Well?' said Kenny. 'You finally got it. Let's have a look then.'

I showed him the piece of paper. When I unfolded it I couldn't believe my eyes. Instead of an ordinary piece of paper, Robbie had given me a twenty pound note! Written clearly in blue ink above the queen's head it said:

**'To the lads from Robbie Kidd.
Get yourself a haircut!'**

'Flippin' Nora!' said Kenny. 'Twenty pounds!'

I gave him a sharp look. 'Don't even think about it,' I said.

Nice One, Sam!

John Goodwin

Illustrated by Clive Goodyer

The huge crowd were up on their feet. 'Penalty! Penalty!' they shouted. The referee blew his whistle and pointed to the spot. The crowd cheered and held their arms aloft. Now surely the winning goal would be scored and for their team it would be triumph yet again. Still their cheering echoed round the stadium and mingled with chants of 'Paggio . . . Paggio.'

Roberto Paggio, the team's captain, stepped forward and placed the ball on the spot. The crowd were quiet now and all the players stood quite still. Paggio too stood still. He looked at the ball then at the goal and then back at the ball again. He shook his hands by his sides and then took three very deliberate steps back. All eyes were on the ball . . .

He ran forward swiftly and hit the ball hard and true as only a great player can. The ball was

right on target and zoomed towards the bottom right corner of the net. It was perfection. Yet a blurred low shape was moving to the same spot too. A blurred shape in green was hurling itself towards the ball. Arms were flung forward and in a rolling mass of ball and gloves and goalkeeper's body the penalty was . . .

I switched off the video and dressed for school. Tuesday is 'can't wait' day. It's straight downstairs. Sneak past Mum's and Amber's bedrooms and don't make a sound on the creaking floorboard to wake the dog. Pull the magazine out of the letter box and stuff your fingers in the letter box flap to stop it shutting to with a crash. Then fly upstairs as fast and quietly as you can clutching the magazine tight in your fist. Close your bedroom door without a sound and then breathe more easily. Open the fingers of your hand for your fist full of football fantasy and magic. For Tuesday is the day of *SCORE* and its free football sticker.

Only it wasn't. Not this Tuesday. The letter box was closed with a tight shut mouth. No football magazine sticking out of its jaws. No sticker to add to the collection.

I stared hard at the letter box half expecting the flap mouth to open at any second and the roll of the magazine to be pushed through. I waited for ages. I waited until my toes were blue with cold and my teeth started to chatter.

There was only one thing to do. I'd have to lever open the flap of the letter box, look through it, and see if the magazine was lying outside on the pavement.

But it wasn't. Not this Tuesday. My fingers slipped on the letter box flap and it shut to with a crash. I opened the door as quietly as I could and set off along the pavement faster than the players come out of the tunnel at the start of a match. I had one target in my view—Goodall's

Paper Shop. I began to run. The trees in Lime Grove were the players of the other team. I passed three and they didn't move a centimetre. I was just too quick for their lumbering branches to catch me. The goal was in sight. I went to round a fourth. This was so easy.

Then the defence showed their dirty play. A huge root of a tree viciously burst through a crack in the pavement. It was a brute of a root deep from the black earth. Then it was round my ankle and pulling me crashing to the ground.

'Penalty . . . penalty!' screamed the crowd. Now I was Roberto Paggio and then I was in green and hurling myself sideways along High Street and straight into Goodall's Paper Shop. My gloved goalkeeper hands were ready to grab that fist full of football stickers. Behind the counter stood Mrs Goodall in her referee's black uniform.

'Steady on, lad,' she said, taking a pencil from behind her ear and licking the end of it.

'I want . . . '

'I know what you want,' she said, licking the pencil for a second time. I have cornflakes for my breakfast and poor old Mrs Goodall has to make do with a lead pencil for hers.

'You came in here last week, didn't you?' she asked as her thick black pencil scrawled the names of houses onto a huge bundle of newspapers.

'Yes,' I said quietly.

'Then you'll know the paper boy delivers your papers.'

'Yes,' I said even quieter.

'So why have you come here?' she asked lifting an even bigger bundle of newspapers onto the shop counter. I just stared at the size of the bundle and no words could find their way onto my lips.

'I know why,' she said without looking at me. 'It's those football stickers . . . isn't it?'

I nodded a silent nod.

'And your stickers are in the magazine which the paper boy has with him.'

It went very quiet in the shop.

'Oh,' I said after a while and took a step back towards the shop door.

'Lucky I've got a spare packet of them,' said Mrs Goodall as she pulled a set of stickers out of her pocket and threw them towards me. I dived forward and caught them  with the best goalkeeper grip I could manage.

 'For me?' I asked her.

'Well, they're not for Michael Owen. Now take them out of my way. I need to get on with these papers.'

I wanted no second telling and was out of the shop in a stride. Once outside I ripped open the packet of stickers with my teeth. It was a four to one chance. Ben  Buck . . . I'd got him. Vinny Capstick . . . everybody's got him ten times over. Two to go. Please PLEASE! I'll do anything if it could be him. Not be rude to Amber for a whole week . . .

promise . . . promise anything if only . . . Georgio Fabrizi . . . oh no . . . he's the worst player ever. And now for the last one. The big one. I can't look. I won't have . . . him. I know I won't. Look now.

YES! WOW! YES! YES!

Look again. Pinch yourself. It is

MIKA TAILER

The sticker everybody wants and **nobody** but **nobody** has got so far. Except me. And I'm going to keep him. Yes . . . you bet I am. Never take my eyes off him. **Mika** the best goalkeeper of all time. **Mika** the greatest footballer ever. **Mika** the only goalkeeper to save three penalties in a world cup final. **Mika my hero**.

I just stood and stared at his face. I had been trying to collect his sticker ever since the magazine had first come out and here he was. I put my finger to the sticker and very carefully let it go right round the shape of his face. Magic! It was just magic.

My finger was coming back to the top of his head for a second time when it sort of jumped off the sticker. It did it by itself. It was like when you touch something burning hot. But my finger wasn't hot at all. It was cold. I looked at Mika's face again and it seemed to be smiling. I know you might think I was dreaming but I tell you . . . his face was smiling.

I looked at the smiling face for ages. Then my eyes started to go blurry and I couldn't see straight . . . I put the sticker carefully into my big trouser pocket making sure that I didn't crease or crumple it. Very slowly I did up the pocket zip so that it wouldn't rip the sticker. Then I set off home making up my mind that I would run all the way there without stopping.

2

Smack! A hand grabbed at me. A hand was at my blazer and pulling me back. I was stopped dead in my tracks. I just froze. Then there was laughing. Laughing coming from behind and in front of me. I know that laughing. I'd know it anywhere. Knocker stepped out in front of me from behind the trees in Lime Grove.

'What we got here then? You've got the wrong badge on our blazer, what a shame,' he said with his face very close to mine.

I tried to pull back but Josh still had his hand on my blazer and he wouldn't let go.

'He's a mummy's boy with the wrong badge on his blazer. What a prat,' said Josh.

'Let go,' I said.

'Have you ever seen anybody run like him?' said Knocker. 'He runs like a spider.'

'Please let go . . . ' I said.

'Spider . . . spider,' shouted Josh and Knocker together in a chant.

'He's a spider man,' shouted Knocker louder than ever.

I felt my hand go down towards my trouser pocket. Down towards that sticker. Then I pulled it back sharply.

'Please don't let them find out about that. Anything but that. Don't let them find out about Mika . . . please,' I said to myself.

Then it went very still. Very quiet. Knocker didn't move or say anything. He just stared at me. Josh's hand wasn't pulling at my blazer quite so tight. But I didn't move. I know their tricks. Mean, vicious tricks. The kind of tricks that do your head in and make you feel stupid and scared. Then Knocker said very quietly, 'Where you going, Spider Man?'

I tried to look away from him, to pull my head away from his stare.

'Nowhere,' I said.

'Nowhere?' repeated Knocker and he turned to face Josh. 'There's no such place,' he said. 'I don't know anybody who comes from nowhere

. . . do you, Josh?' Knocker began to laugh again.

'I know what comes from nowhere,' said Josh.

'What's that?' said Knocker.

'Spiders . . . spiders come from nowhere. Smelly little spiders. Nowhere is the only place they can live.'

Now they were both laughing. Rocking about and laughing at their own stupid jokes. I knew I had to make a move. They would only be off guard for a second. It was now or never.

I ducked low. Josh's hand came away from gripping me.

'Watch it. Spider on the loose,' shouted Knocker.

Josh's hand was on my blazer again and pulling it tight. I ducked even lower and strained forward. Still he held on to me. Still I pulled. Now there was a ripping noise. My blazer was ripping. I didn't care. Not one bit. Let it rip all it liked. If it wasn't for stupid blazers none of this would have ever happened in the first place. They'd have had no reason to pick on me. Instead it would have been somebody else.

'Spider spider!' shouted Knocker as he stepped out to block my way. But I started to run. I was like a forward on the wing. I could swerve past him. I knew I could. I kept low to the ground. He lurched at me with both arms outstretched. A giant foul lurch. But I ducked too low for him and then I was past and out into the open spaces of the wide pitch.

'Spider on the loose,' shouted Josh. 'Where are you going? You left half your blazer behind.'

In his fist he had a torn piece of my blazer pocket which he waved in the air. But by now I was over the halfway line and heading for home. Soon the goal would be in sight. When I saw it I dived inside the house and ran straight upstairs to my bedroom. I took off the ripped blazer and stuffed it under the mattress of my bunk bed. It made the mattress a bit lumpy with a bump in the middle. With a few belly flop goalie dives on top of it the lump almost went down to nothing. Unless you looked really close you couldn't tell it was under there at all.

What really mattered was that my trouser pocket was not ripped at all. I undid the zip to see the sticker was still safe and sound. And what's more Mika's face was still smiling at me.

3

Kick the ball. Kick it hard. Kick it straight. Kick it at the third brick in the wall. Think the brick is Vinny Capstick. Pass it to Vinny with the side of your foot. Don't toe end it. Make it accurate. Vinny passes it straight back. A one–two pass. Control it and then off down the wing. Side step one. Side step two and the goal is in sight. Steady now . . . take aim. Hit the goal below the drainpipe.

Our garden is small. In fact a stamp you post on a letter is bigger than our garden. But it's good for having a kick around. It's got a high fence round it to stop big bullies with giant fists and stupid laughs picking on you.

Now for a bit of heading. Throw the ball up. Just a metre or so. Head straight through the ball. Don't close your eyes. Hit it with your forehead. I hate this bit. Really hate it. The ball

seems so hard and I always miss it. Come on
. . . if you are going to be a striker . . . a real
striker, you'll have to learn how to head the
ball. Missed it. I closed my eyes when I
shouldn't have done. Perhaps I am a spider, a
useless hopeless spider just like Knocker says I
am. There to remind me how bad at heading I
was when I didn't need reminding at all was
Tara. She's the girl next door who sometimes
peeps through a little gap in the fence. She
spies on me. I wish she'd got better things to
do.

'Missed it. It's no good closing your eyes like
that. You should have scored from that close,'
she said in that squeaky voice of hers.

I tried to ignore her but still she went on
about it.

'You're scared of it, aren't you? Scared of

heading it. You won't be a real footballer if you can't head it.'

'I can head it, so there.'

'Go on then . . . let's see you.'

I turned my back on Tara's peeping face coming through the gap in the fence and tried to shut her out of my mind. I undid the zip of my trouser pocket. The sticker lay neatly at the bottom of the pocket. It was like the pocket was made for that sticker. It fitted perfectly. I took the sticker out and looked hard at it. It wasn't creased or crumpled or dirty. It was just shiny. I looked hard at Mika's face. 'Come on, Mika,' I said to myself. 'We'll show Miss Squeaky Voice a thing or two.'

My finger was going round the shape of the face without me even having to put it there. For the second time it was coming back to the top of his head when my finger jumped off the picture. It was just like it did before outside Goodall's Paper Shop. Just like before I felt burning hot. Only this time it was my leg that was hot. My right leg was burning. It was burning with Mika power.

Something was guiding my leg towards the football as it lay on the ground. Something was pulling my leg back very slowly indeed. Then forward it went like a rocket. It hit the ball hard and true. *Whack* went the ball straight into the fence and *whack* as it rebounded into the opposite fence. Then the ball took off. Straight into the air it zoomed. *Higher* and *higher* it climbed, heading straight up. I stood and stared at it until it was a tiny dot in the sky. It went out of sight and I thought that was the last time I'd see it. But I was wrong. The tiny dot appeared again but all the time getting bigger. The ball was falling back to earth like a meteorite falling from the sky.

The ball hit the ground at an amazing speed right next to my feet and then went up again. It hit next door's roof and then began to slow down. Now the ball was moving in slow motion back towards our garden. It hovered just above my head and then finally landed into my outstretched hands.

I was gobsmacked. I turned it round slowly making sure it wasn't some alien spacecraft from outer space full of a deadly virus. But it was the same old ball sure enough with scuffed black and white patterns on it. I was still looking at it and up at the sky when I heard that squeaky voice again.

'How did you do that, Sam?' she asked.

'What?' I said.

'That zap kick.'

'Oh that.'

'It was huge.'

'It was nothing,' I said. 'Just my usual skill.'

Football is a tactical game. Keep it tight when you're winning is something you should always remember. So with that in mind I bounced the ball once at my feet and headed for our back door.

Tara shouted, 'That wasn't your usual skill, Sam. Nothing like it. That was just . . . *WOW*!'

I pretended I hadn't heard her. It was time to watch my favourite football video of Mika's famous penalty saves of the World Cup Final. Whilst that was on I was trying to make sense of all that had happened out there in the back garden.

4

I ran onto the field in a rush. I'd show them this time. I did a spring up and down the pitch before most of the others were out of the changing room. No more miskicking for me. No more feeble tries to head the ball. I was a striker to be reckoned with. A striker that could kick a ball into orbit. I could be in *The Guinness Book of Records*. A famous striker with inter-galactic footballing skills.

Then the rest came out. I heard Josh giggling at me as I ran up and down the touchline but I didn't care. He'd soon see something that would take that stupid grin off his face.

Mr Brailsford gathered us round and picked two teams like he always did.

'Charlton, Wayne, Woody, Daniel, Josh, Edward, and Ben . . . '

Mr Brailsford's picking was just about complete.

'James, Ryan, and . . . Jack.'

There were only two players left in our class without a team. One a giant of a boy with size ten boots and the other a skinny little lad with inter-galactic ambitions.

'Sir . . . what about me?' said the boy with size tens.

'Oh . . . you, Knocker.'

'Yes, sir.'

It went very quiet for a bit and then Mr Brailsford turned to me and Knocker.

'Would you believe it, I almost forgot you two,' he said.

I didn't know what was going on. I thought perhaps we were going to get the red card before we'd even started. Then he said, 'You'll both just have to play in the same team, won't you?'

Knocker glared at me and said, 'Oh, sir . . . can't he play in the other team?'

'No,' said Mr Brailsford. 'I just said you will both play in the same team.'

'But he's useless. A wet wimpy spider with . . . '

But Mr Brailsford didn't let Knocker finish his sentence.

'If I hear another word, Paul, you won't play at all. You can spend the lesson in the changing room. Is that clear?'

Knocker knew it was very clear and that when Mr Brailsford called him Paul and not by his nickname it was serious. Mr Brailsford was a teacher who kept his word.

We kicked off. I positioned myself as a striker and ran up towards the other team's penalty area. I ran fast and hard and found myself with a bit of open space around me. I eyed up their goalie . . . Josh. He wasn't that good. He only went in goal because nobody else in their team wanted to. Surely I could put a shot past him and find the back of the net. All I needed was one good chance. One neat pass from midfield, a quick dart up the pitch and the shot was on. We could be one–nil up, no sweat.

I waited for ages in that open space by myself. Nothing happened. No neat pass came from midfield. No pass came at all. I might as well have been on a different planet for all the part I played in the match. Most of the play happened in the other half of the field and we were soon two–nil down.

When we did get the ball Knocker had it. It was as if it was glued to the end of his size tens and there was nobody else in the team but him. He ran all over the pitch. He barged and pushed, then ran some more, lost control of the ball and shot miles wide of the goal.

Out of nowhere we got a free kick. Mr Brailsford blew his whistle hard.

'Free kick,' he said. 'You take it, Sam. Give it a big kick upfield.' He placed the ball on the ground.

'Not him,' shouted Knocker. 'He can't kick his way out of a bag of chips.'

Some of the kids began to giggle and I could hear Josh far away in the goal with his loud stupid laughing. The more he laughed the worse it was. I felt all stiff in my back just like the time when he grabbed my blazer.

'Don't take any notice of the rest, Sam,' said Mr Brailsford. 'Just give it one big kick.'

I looked at the ball and tried not to think about Knocker or Josh or being a spider. I tried really hard. But somehow I couldn't do it. I couldn't block them out. My foot hit the ground in front of the ball and instead of it flying high up into the air upfield it just trickled forward a few centimetres and then stopped. I could hear booing coming from Josh in goal way upfield. Loud echoing booing.

Mr Brailsford blew his whistle sharply.

'Half time. Change ends . . . and cut out that booing.'

I ran off the field. Not in tears but pretty close to tears and my legs felt all wobbly. I went into the changing room, took something out of my trouser pocket and put it into my football shorts pocket. It would be a risk. It might go very wrong but there was nothing else I could do. I just couldn't stand the thought of that booing happening again.

The second half started. I ran upfield just like before and just like before nobody passed the ball to me. The other team scored and we were three–nil down. It was hopeless. I began to think that run off the field and into the changing room was a complete waste of time. It just didn't seem worth it.

I could feel the sticker that was hidden in my shorts pocket. I traced round where I thought Mika's face would be. I was so busy doing it that I hadn't noticed the ball roll towards me. A perfect pass from midfield. What I'd waited for all game. But I just stood and stared at the ball. Behind me the rest were shouting and yelling. Their cries were getting closer.

'Kick it. Kick it up. Go for goal. Sam, kick it up.'

If I didn't do something soon it would be too late.

I ran forward three steps and looked at the goal. It seemed miles away. Surely I couldn't shoot for goal from this far back. Behind me the rest of the players were so close. The ground was shaking as two size ten boots pounded the turf a few metres away.

It was now or never. I put my hand on the

sticker and felt my leg burn just like before. The burning leg pulled itself slowly back. Too slowly. I could see the studs of Knocker's size tens out of the corner of my eyes. My leg went forward at galactic speed. It struck the ball at seventy miles an hour. Off zoomed the ball goalwards. It didn't head for the stars like last time but was a hard low volley right on target.

Josh saw it coming. He wasn't booing now. No way. That volley had shut him up for sure. He placed himself in the centre of the goal and watched it like a hawk. His hands and body were ready to block its movement when the right moment came. Yet the ball was swerving and gathering speed as it travelled through the air.

Faster and faster it went. I wanted to shout out. To tell everybody that it was impossible to stop a shot like this one. That Josh better move

out of the way before he was killed. Before I could say a word the ball was near the goal and heading for the top corner of the net. Yet it missed the net and crashed into the goalpost. Crunch went the post and down fell the net as the goalpost was broken into two different pieces.

All the players stood on the pitch and looked at the broken mess. Mr Brailsford was leading Josh away from the tangled web of net and post and Josh was scratching his head in a daze. I just stared at it all. Had I done this? Had one kick of the ball caused all this? I couldn't cheer or shout out or say how good it was to hit a shot like that. I should have been dancing round the pitch with my shirt pulled over my head like they do on the telly. Instead I just felt numb. It was like a hurricane had struck.

'What a mess,' said Charlton.

'What a strike,' said Mr Brailsford. 'The strike of the century. I've never seen a kick like it. We shall all have to wear crash hats next. How did you do a kick like that, Sam?'

For some questions it's best not to try and find an answer.

5

After school I went to the school library for a bit. I wanted to let all the rest of the kids go home before I walked out through the school gates. It's best that way. Then there's no Knocker to meet on the way home.

It was gone half past four by the time I lifted the catch of the gate and stepped into our back garden. Straight away I heard a voice. It was Tara. I could even see her lips moving in the gap in the fence.

'When did a referee first use a whistle in a football match?' said the lips.

'What?'

'When did a referee first use a whistle in a football match?' she repeated.

'I dunno.'

'1878,' she said.

I took another step towards our back door.

'You been playing football, Sam?'

'Yeah.'

'Are there any girls playing in your team?'

'No.'

'Why not?'

'School rules. No girls.'

'That's stupid rules . . . girls are as good as boys any day.'

I looked at the lips in the gap and then I said, 'I scored a goal today.'

She drew in a sharp breath and then she said, 'You didn't.'

'Did.'

'How'd you do that?' she asked.

'I just ki—'

I stopped in the middle of the word. Could I tell her? Could I really say all about Mika and the sticker and all that? I began to speak again.

'I hit it with . . . '

She didn't let me finish what I wanted to say . . . not choose the right words.

'Did you zap kick it?' she asked.

'Yeah . . . I zap kicked it,' I said and took

another couple of steps towards our back door. My hand was on the door handle.

'Don't go in, Sam,' said Tara loudly.

'Why not?'

'Cos . . . I wanted to warn you . . . she found your blazer.'

My hand came away from the door handle.

'What?' I said. 'How do you know about that?'

'Your mum was shouting about it, right out here. Saying that it was all ripped. "Ruined," she said. I could hear her. She hasn't half got a loud voice your mum.'

I turned to the gap in the fence with the lips showing through.

'I wanted to tell you,' said Tara. 'So you'd know. But your mum has gone out till later. She's gone to take Amber to 'er dancin' lessons. Back about six.'

It went quiet for a bit.

'You can come and wait in my house, Sam, if you like. We could have a game of the football quiz. That one I got for Christmas.'

I didn't go round to Tara's. I just wanted

to be by myself for a bit. What I needed was to try and sort a few things out inside my head. Time to think. I went up to my bedroom.

The blazer was lying on my bed. The patch where the pocket should have been was facing the top. It was all my mother's fault anyway. How could she have put the wrong school badge on that blazer at the beginning? A blue badge with a castle on it instead of the red rose for our school? How could you get them mixed up? But mixed up they were and Knocker and Josh picked on me the very first day I started at that school.

'Look at 'im.'

' 'E's got the wrong badge on 'is blazer.'

'What a thicko.'

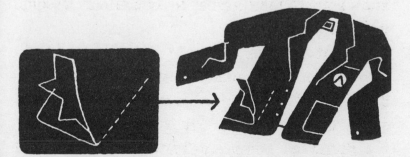

I couldn't touch that blazer on top of my bed. I couldn't go anywhere near it. It came to six o'clock and then half past. Still no sign of Mum or Amber. When they did come in much later they were all happy that Amber had won first prize in a big dance show and the blazer was forgotten for a while.

6

I waited for Knocker to hit next. After I smashed down the goalpost he'd be waiting to pick on me. He was bound to. The next two days it was very quiet. Too quiet.

Then it began. On Monday pages were ripped out of one of my school books. Nobody saw it happen. On Tuesday somebody threw paint all over our front door. Nobody saw it happen. On Wednesday somebody slashed the tyres on my bike. Guess what? Nobody saw it happen.

Thursday was school football. I tried to go sick.

'I can't play, Mr Brailsford.'

'Why not, Sam?'

'Bad leg, sir.'

'Have you got a sick note?'

'No, sir.'

'You know the rules. No sick note, no excuse. Get changed.'

I knew something was going to happen. It did. I turned my back for a few minutes in the changing room and my bag went missing. What was far, far worse was that in the bag were my football shorts and in the shorts pocket was my sticker.

Disaster.

Yes, this was a disaster.

How could I have been so stupid?

'Mr Brailsford . . . my bag is missing.'

'It can't be. Search the changing room.'

'I've searched twice. The bag had— '

'What? What did the bag have in it?'

I paused. I couldn't tell him. No way.

'It had . . . my . . . er . . . football kit in it,' I mumbled.

Mr Brailsford came into the changing room. He looked at all our class.

'Sam's bag has gone missing,' he said. 'Look in all your stuff . . . under the seats . . . in the lockers. Let's see if we can find it.'

The changing room was searched. No bag was found. Mr Brailsford looked at the class.

'No bag, no football lesson,' he said.

'Oh, sir,' said most of the class.

But Mr Brailsford was not shifting.

'If somebody has stolen Sam's bag they are in big trouble. The bag has all his football kit in it. This may be a matter for the police. If one of you here is a thief I want to know who it is.'

It went very quiet. Mr Brailsford was looking at the class.

'I am going to ask you one at a time. Tell me if you know anything about this.'

It was still silent. He spoke to each of us in turn.

'Jamie?'

'No, sir.'

'Ravi?'

'No, sir.'

Mr Brailsford came to face Knocker. He called him by his real name.

'Paul?'

Knocker didn't move at all.

'No, sir,' he said.

I was getting angry. Of course Knocker knew something about it. The slashed tyres, the ripped books, and the wet paint. Oh yes, Mr Big knew plenty about all those. He knew plenty about my missing kit. But did he know about the sticker? If he did I was in real trouble. Only finding out the truth was something else.

Mr Brailsford reached Josh.

'Josh?'

Josh looked down at the ground. He started to bite his lip.

'Josh, do you know something about this?'

Josh mumbled something under his breath.

'What was that?' asked Mr Brailsford.

'No,' said Josh.

'Are you sure?'

Josh bit his lip again. It went very quiet. Then suddenly Charlton jumped up.

'It was Knocker and Josh,' shouted Charlton. 'They did it.'

Now Knocker was angry. 'You liar. I never did anything.'

But Charlton stood his ground. 'They did . . . they did . . . look.'

Charlton pointed up towards the top locker. Everybody's eyes looked up.

'I can't see anything,' said Mr Brailsford.

'They hid his bag on top of the locker. I saw them do it,' said Charlton.

Mr Brailsford climbed up onto a bench. He reached up high and pulled out something. It was covered with cobwebs and dirt. He looked at me.

'Is this your bag, Sam?'

'Yes.'

'Check it over.'

I opened the bag. My boots, shirt, and shorts were inside.

'Is everything OK?' asked Mr Brailsford.

I felt the shorts again. My hand went towards the pockets. Everyone was looking at me. I could feel their eyes staring at

me. I daren't let everybody know about the sticker. I pulled my hand back.

'It's OK,' I said.

Mr Brailsford looked straight at Knocker.

'Did you do this?' he asked.

'He did. He did. He's got it in for Sam. Him and Josh,' said Charlton.

'Yes they have. They always pick on him,' shouted the rest of the class.

'Well, they won't any more,' said Mr Brailsford. He looked at Knocker and Josh.

'Get changed out of your kit, you two. No football for you two today.'

They got changed and Mr Brailsford marched them out of the changing room to wait outside his office. Now I was safe. I reached into the pocket of my football shorts. The sticker was still there. I began to breathe more easily again.

I'd won the battle of the football kit thanks to Charlton, but there was still a war going on. A Knocker and Josh war. They wouldn't take any prisoners. They'd show no mercy. I waited for them to strike again. It could be any place and at any time. I had to be on my guard.

Two days later there was a knock on our door. I went to answer it. I opened the door but there was nobody there. I looked up the road both ways. Nobody was in sight.

'A Knocker trick,' I said to myself.

I went to shut the door. Just as I did I saw something on the ground. I went to pick it up. It was an old football shirt that had been cut and ripped and smeared with dirt. Pinned to it was a piece of paper which said:

We are going to get you, Spider.

It wasn't Knocker that struck next but the flu. It hit our school harder than a brick thrown through a window. Kids were sick everywhere. Some puked up in assembly. Some had to be taken home in teachers' cars. Knocker and Josh got it. I couldn't believe my luck. But my luck didn't last. Knocker came back two days later.

I tried to keep cool. I kept my distance from Knocker and went to the library for a bit of shelter. I was hiding behind a big thick book on dinosaurs when Charlton came into the library.

'Sam,' he shouted.

'Quiet please,' said the librarian.

'Guess what?' said Charlton.

'QUIET PLEASE!' shouted the librarian.

Charlton came closer and started to whisper.

'You've been picked.'

'What?' I asked.

'For the school team. Loads of kids are still off sick. So Mr Brailsford said you're in.'

It was true. We both went down to the notice board outside the changing rooms and there it was.

Sam Wicklow, it said in Mr Brailsford's neat handwriting. In a day's time I would be playing my very first match for the under 13s in a cup match against St John's.

Or would I? There was another name written on the team-sheet.

Paul Osborn.

Paul Osborn alias Knocker. I thought of the football shirt thrown at our door. Did I really want to play after all?

Back at home after school Tara was lying in wait.

'How many times have England beaten Germany in the last hundred years, Sam?'

'Dunno, Tara.'

'Yes you do.'

'I said I don't know.'

She glared at me with her spying eye through the gap in the fence.

'I spy with my little eye,' she said.

'I haven't got time for baby games, Tara.'

'Something beginning with "s".'

I tried to ignore her.

'"S" for scared. Who's scared, Sam?' she said.

I stopped walking across the garden.

'You should play, Sam. You've got to play.'

I turned towards the fence.

'What you talking about?'

'Charlton told me all about it,' she said.

I went inside and slammed the door behind me. I wasn't going to let Tara get to me. But I knew in my heart she was right.

It was the day of my first school match. Mr Brailsford was holding a pep talk in the changing room.

'This is the big one,' he said. 'It's a cup match. If we lose we'll be knocked out. It's as simple as that. But we are not going to think of defeat. Oh no. We are going for victory. We're going to win today, aren't we?'

All our voices spoke as one. 'Yes, sir.'

Mr Brailsford looked across our sea of faces.

'Good . . . good,' he said. 'We've made just one team change . . . Sam is a striker. Now all of you remember there are other players in our team besides yourself. Try not to be selfish with the ball. A winning team is a passing team.'

We began to change. Then Mr Brailsford piled a big heap of red and white striped football shirts in the middle of the room.

'New shirts . . . for the match,' he said.

Hands pulled at the pile and soon eager young players poured out of the changing room to begin a pre-match warm up. I was still in the changing room staring at the one shirt that was left. Was that shirt really for me? It was impossible. Knocker was right. I couldn't kick my way out of a bag of chips. I'd better tell Mr Brailsford straight away so he could find a substitute for me. Then Mr Brailsford came into the changing room.

'Come on you, Sam. Get your shirt on,' he said.

'It . . . won't fit,' I lied.

'How do you know . . . you haven't tried it on yet.'

'But, sir, I . . . '

'No buts . . . there isn't time. We're ready to start the match,' he said and went out onto the pitch.

I picked up the new shirt. It felt so sleek and shiny. An idea came to me. The sleeves of the shirt were quite tight. Maybe I could tuck the Mika sticker in the cuff of the sleeve and rub it when I needed a zap kick. That would give me power. I just hoped it wouldn't be power out of control and break the goalposts like last time . . .

'Sam . . . come on, Sam . . . or we shall start without you,' came a cry from outside.

I pulled the shirt on, tucked the sticker inside the sleeve and with my fingers crossed ran out of the changing room and onto the pitch.

In the first half they pounded our defences. Time and time again the ball was crossed with corner after corner but somehow they failed to find the net.

I watched it all from a distance and stood by myself in the centre circle waiting in vain for the ball to come my way. But it never did.

'Get yourself in the game, Sam,' shouted Mr Brailsford from the touchline. 'Go and get the ball . . . don't stand about waiting for it to come to you.'

He was shouting at everybody and beginning to lose his voice. I tried to run but I was scared the sticker would fall out of my sleeve and fall into the mud of the pitch. I just gave up. Then

Knocker had the ball and sped down the pitch like a headless chicken.

'Pass it . . . pass it . . . pass it!' shouted Mr Brailsford. But Knocker held on to it and dribbled away. He cleared one player and a second but he just couldn't stop himself showing off. As usual he tried to dribble it past one opponent too many and lost control of the ball. Our attack broke down and their pounding started all over again.

At last the whistle went for half time and Mr Brailsford gathered us round for what should have been another pep talk. Only we had no pep and he had no voice. So we each sucked half an orange and stood around feeling lost.

The second half began with a freak bit of luck. We caught them napping. From the kick off the ball was booted high up in the air up towards their goal. I forgot about my sticker falling out and sprinted off upfield. There was Knocker by my side running too and a whole gaggle of us charging down the pitch like a lot of sheep being chased by a dog. The ball came down and skidded off one of the St John's defenders for a corner. Our first of the match.

Charlton took the corner, a good one fired just out of reach of their keeper. Up jumped the gaggle. Red and white stripes mingled with yellow. Their heads strained towards the spinning ball. Defenders and attackers struggling desperately to make first contact with the ball.

One tall and sometimes selfish attacker was centimetres higher than the rest. Knocker's head was so close to the ball and an open net beckoned. His head pulled back, poised to strike and missed. Yes, missed the ball completely. The gaggle began to plummet to the earth. Bodies sagged. The ball fell too and struck the chest of Knocker's red and white striped shirt. I could see it spinning in slow motion towards the black mesh of the goal. A goalie's desperate outstretched hand tried to grasp it but the ball was just out of reach. Still spinning it went over the goalie's head and landed firmly in the back of the net.

'Yeees!' shouted Knocker raising his arms aloft, fists clenched and eyes tight shut. We soaked in the triumph. One–nil up. The tide had turned. It was enough to make Mr Brailsford find his voice again.

'Back,' he shouted. 'Back, all of you in defence. Keep it tight. Make them fight for it.'

So back we went and their bombardment started all over again.

Zoom came the ball . . . out went a foot as we cleared the goal line again and again. A big gaggle of bodies bunched in our penalty area. They should have scored loads of goals. But they didn't. Surely it was only a matter of time before they scored. Somebody had to do something. Somebody who had not really played any part in the game and had hardly kicked the ball yet . . . The words Mr Brailsford had said at the start of the match were pounding in my head.

'Wear your shirts with pride.'

It was up to me. It was time for me to show some pride. To stop playing like a scared wimp and show some pride. The next time the ball came anywhere near me I'd do it. Mika wouldn't let me down. My hand was ready on the sticker. Ready to trace round his shape. Ready for him to smile and for me to have the huge power in my leg and crack the ball all the length of the pitch and into their goal. If I kicked from near our goal it would be safe enough not to break the goalposts. Then we'd be two–nil up . . . the game in the bag. Victory was ours for the taking.

They won another corner. This was it. The moment I'd waited for all match. I positioned myself on the goal line, let my finger go round Mika's face as the ball was curving high through the air towards me. My finger was back to the top of the head for the second time and I waited for my leg to go strong and powerful. Only it didn't seem to . . . The ball was almost on me when I began to jump. Up in the air I went, propelled by Mika power. Higher and higher I climbed. I had a sudden panic. Maybe I was going into orbit like the ball in our back garden. Look out, Jupiter . . . here I come.

My arms were hot. Mika power was in my arms. They shot out like a spring uncoiled as I caught the ball just before it hit the back of the net.

'Penalty! Penalty!' screamed the opposition.

I fell to the ground clutching the ball.

'You caught the ball . . . but you're not the goalie,' said a quiet voice. 'You've given away a penalty . . . and now we'll lose the game.'

I heard what they were saying but my legs were out of control. The power had taken over. I was up on my feet clutching the ball at my chest. The ref's whistle was blowing but I took no notice.

'Penalty, Sam,' shouted Mr Brailsford. 'Put the ball down.'

But I didn't. I ran two steps with it. Now everybody was shouting.

'Put the ball down.'

Still I ignored them. I pulled my arm back and hurled the ball forward miles high in the air. As I did so something fell out of the sleeve of my shirt. But I paid no attention to it. I found myself shouting. It was as if I had no control over what I was saying. The words just came out of my mouth by themselves.

'Go on. Go for it. Chase the ball. Let's have a goal. Go for it, Knocker. Go for goal.'

Only Knocker didn't go for goal. Instead he was looking at something on the ground. It was my sticker. It had fallen out of my sleeve. Before I had time to think Knocker bent down and grabbed the sticker in his hand and then crumpled it in his fist.

'Give that back,' I said.

But he wasn't listening.

'You stupid spider. You've ruined our chance of winning the game.' Then he pulled his fist back and punched me in the face.

8

There was blood streaming from my nose. The referee ran towards Knocker at speed. He blew his whistle hard and pulled out a red card.

'Off the field,' he shouted. 'Now.'

Mr Brailsford came running onto the pitch and marched Knocker off towards the changing room. The St John's players began to boo and laugh.

'Off . . . off . . . off,' they chanted.

The referee ran up to me and gave me tissues to wipe away the blood from my nose.

'You better have a sit down,' he said.

'I'm OK,' I said.

It was true. Even though the blood was still pouring out of my nose it didn't seem to hurt at all.

It took ten minutes to restart the game. The

referee placed the ball on the penalty spot. I turned my back. I couldn't watch. It was all my fault and there was nothing I could do about it. It went very quiet. Then I heard feet running along the ground. There was a thud as a foot struck the ball and then a cheer. I didn't need anyone to tell me that St John's had scored.

The ref blew his whistle soon afterwards and we all trooped off the pitch. We got changed in silence. I had thrown away our chance of victory in one stupid moment. The match was a draw. We'd have to have a replay . . .

There was no sign of Knocker. I could see my crumpled sticker in his fist in my mind. I had to get it back off him. But how was I going to do that?

When I got home Tara was waiting. She was up to her usual spying tricks with her nose poked through the gap in our fence.

'What you done to your nose?' she asked.

'Nothing.'

'What you done to your voice?' she asked.

'Nothing.'

'But it's different. It's gone deeper.'

I went into the house and up to my bedroom. Mum and Amber were out as usual. I looked at my face in the mirror to see what damage Knocker's fist had done. There was no blood on my nose but something was strange. My face looked different. It seemed to have grown longer. It was weird. I wondered if it was a trick. Was it Amber messing about? Had she got one of those mirrors like you get in a fairground and put it in my bedroom to scare me?

I ran downstairs to look in another mirror. Different mirror but the same strange face. I began to panic. My heart was racing. Then I remembered concussion. That's what you get when you have a knock on your head and you go all wobbly. Wobbly face means wobbly concussion. That was it. I'd got it sorted. The best thing for concussion was to lie down and take it easy. So that's what I did.

I must have been asleep for ages because when I woke up it was just getting light the next morning. Birds were singing outside the window. It was when I sat up that I first saw them. My legs. Could they be my legs? They had grown. Oh yes, they had grown so that they stuck out nearly to touch my bedroom wall. But it wasn't just my legs that had grown. Oh no. So had my hands. They were huge. My arms and head and chest were ginormous . . . In fact all of me was twice the size it should have been. And there was something else. I looked at the long legs again that seemed to belong to me and saw they were covered in hairs. Thick black hairs also sprouted out of my armpits like a tropical jungle. I had grown a man's body.

As I sat in my bed which was now far too small for me my eyes went towards the mirror on the wall. The same mirror that last night had shown me a long long face. At that moment I knew what had happened. For now I saw not my own face but that of Mika Tailer. By some weird trick I had taken the body of a world famous goalkeeper. It seemed that Mika power had grown so strong it had taken over my whole body. All of me was Mika. There was nothing left of Sam. WOW! Or had I? This couldn't really happen, could it? Was I still suffering from concussion?

I reached into a drawer and pulled out a video. I slotted the video into the TV. Maybe the video could tell me the truth. I looked again in the mirror and back towards the video as it was playing. There could be no mistake. The face in the mirror and the face on the video were exactly the same. Same hair, nose, eyes, mouth. Same man.

'Sam.'

It was my mother's voice.

'Sam!' she shouted. 'Come on, you'll be late for school.'

School? How could I go to school in the body of the world's best goalie? I wouldn't be able to fit my knees under my desk to start with. Trying to pull a boy's ripped blazer over my new body was going to be fun. What would I put on my feet?

'Sam? Are you OK?' asked my mother.

'Yes,' I mumbled trying to make my voice sound normal.

There was a pause. A nasty sort of pause then she asked, 'Are you feeling ill?'

I had to do something about my voice. I pushed my pillow up against my mouth hoping it would sound different and said, 'I'll be out in a minute.'

There was another nasty pause then I could see the bedroom door handle moving.

'Open the door, Sam,' she said.

The door of the bedroom sometimes sticks shut and I just hoped she wouldn't be able to open it. If it did open how was I going to explain to her that her only son had changed into a grown man overnight?

I was saved by Amber.

'Mum, what time is it?' she growled from her bedroom.

'Time you were at school,' said my mother.

'Mum . . . did you wash my PE kit?'

'Yes.'

'Where did you put it?'

'It's downstairs.'

'Mum, could you get it for me?'

I heard my mother grumble and then her footsteps going down the stairs and into the kitchen. I reckon I had less than two minutes. I pushed the bedroom door open and ran down the stairs, taking two steps at a time with ease with my new long legs. On a hook in the hall I saw the long black coat Dad used to wear before he left us. It would be better than walking about in pyjamas that were ten sizes too small for me. I pulled it over my shoulders and tied its belt firmly round my waist. His wellington boots were also in the hall so I slipped my feet into them. Then I could hear my mother coming out of the kitchen still grumbling. I ran to the front door, opened it, stepped through and closed it firmly behind me. With giant strides I stepped out into our back garden.

Tara had started her spy watch early. I caught sight of her face in the gap in the fence. She was staring straight at me with her mouth wide open. It opened and closed like a goldfish's mouth. But I was in no mood for goldfish. By my foot was a football which had got left out days before. I just couldn't resist it. I pulled back my giant foot in the wellington boot. It caught the ball perfectly. The ball zoomed off like a cannon-ball. It hit our gate right in the middle. There was a crunch, a splintering of wood, and the gate fell off its hinges onto the ground. The ball bounced high up into the air and disappeared from sight.

Trying not to look at Tara I stepped out into the street and away from our house. But where was I going? What could I do now?

9

Out in the street everything seemed to be a bit smaller than usual. I could see right over walls which used to tower above me. The pavement seemed narrower and walking along it was much easier. Perhaps being trapped in a man's body was not so bad after all. People walked past and didn't even notice me. I even put a smile on my face.

In the next street a few kids were waiting for the school bus. I walked casually towards them. Then it started.

'It is,' said one tiny kid.

'Isn't,' said a girl with ginger hair.

'Is,' repeated the tiny kid.

I looked over towards them and stopped. I put a giant smile on my face, held up my giant hand and waved at them.

'Hi,' I said in a deep voice.

'Cor. It is him,' said the ginger girl.

'Go on ask him,' said another kid.

'Ask him what?'

'Ask him if he's Mika Tailer.'

'I'm not. You ask him.'

I smiled and waved my hand again. The ginger girl giggled and then asked, 'Excuse me are you . . . ?'

'Yes,' I said. 'I'm Mika.'

'Paper . . . get his autograph,' said the ginger girl.

'Yeah,' said the tiny kid.

'Yeah,' repeated all the rest of the kids at the bus stop. They all scurried about opening school bags and searching in pockets for pens and paper. A few seconds later the ginger girl thrust a pen and paper towards me. I smiled at her. This was crazy. I was even beginning to think like Mika.

'What's your name?' I asked her.

'Bethany,' she said.

So I wrote

Then I did the same for Ben and Alice and James and Winston. I wrote Mika till my fingers ached. At the end of the queue stood the tiny kid holding open his maths book.

'Can you sign there?' he asked.

'What, in your maths book?'

'Yeah. I've got nothing else for you to write in,' he said.

So I put a big *Mika* at the top of the page and walked off with a spring in my step.

I found my feet taking me towards the street where Knocker lived.

'Yeah. Why not?' I said to myself. 'Why not give him a surprise visit?'

I reckoned that he had to be at home. After punching me like he did Mr Brailsford would have had him suspended from school. Surely he'd be at his house.

I was right. When I got outside Knocker's

151

house I looked up to the top windows. I could see him through the window playing on his computer. Well, wouldn't he just love to get a visit from a world famous goalkeeper? I stood and watched him for ages and then I saw his mother come out of the side door of the house. She climbed into her car and drove off through the front gates. I watched her go all the way along the road and out of sight. My eyes flicked back towards Knocker. He was in the house alone. I was sure of that. It was a perfect opportunity. For the first time in my life I wasn't afraid of him. If I could now look over brick walls that usually towered miles above my head then surely I could look down at Knocker. For the very first time I was bigger than him. I had bigger legs and arms and feet and bigger fists. I had a bigger brain. Now for the first time I could make him grovel. At last it was his turn to be scared.

I walked calmly across the road. My giant legs strolled through the gates of his house. I raised my huge fist up to knock on the side door. It was at that moment that I saw the side door had been left open. All I had to do was to push the door a little and step inside and make a dream come true.

Yet I hesitated. Could I really do it? I might have a man's body but did I have a man's courage? I could feel those long legs begin to wobble and shake.

'Come on, Sam. You've got to do it. You've got to,' I told myself and with one stride I walked into the house.

I climbed slowly up the stairs of the house. This was spooky. I didn't feel right about being here. I mean, how would I feel if someone did the same to me? But that voice inside me was pulling me on.

I climbed the last stair and stood right outside his bedroom. I could hear the sound of his computer game as he zapped another space-ship of aliens. This was stupid. What was I going to do when I got into his bedroom? Beat him? No way. I'd have to speak to him. But what would I say?

'I'm Mika, I want to talk to you?'

That would be stupid. I took a step back from the door and looked down the stairs. Could I creep away without him knowing that I'd even been there? But what then? I'd be trapped into Mika's body for ever with no way out.

A second later I stepped into his room. I saw the connection from his computer game was in a socket by the door. I reached over to it and snatched the connection out of the socket. Immediately the picture on the computer screen shrank. Then it disappeared altogether as the screen went blank. Knocker swivelled round in his chair and he saw me for the first time. He had the strangest expression on his face that I have ever seen. I took another step into the room.

'Hello, Paul Osborn,' I said.

His face went very white.

'You know who I am,' I said.

'Yes,' he mumbled.

'You've got something of mine,' I said.

He was looking at me like I was a ghost. I had to ask him again.

'You've got something that belongs to me,' I repeated.

'What?' he said.

'You have a sticker of me,' I said.

'What?' he repeated.

I held out my giant hand which he looked at closely.

'Give me that sticker, Paul,' I said.

'Yes,' he said slowly like I had a strange power over him. Then he pulled open a drawer in his computer desk and pulled out a crumpled piece of card.

'Thank you,' I said and opened out my hand to make it even bigger.

He dropped the crumpled card into the palm of my hand. The long fingers of my other hand picked up the crumple. Immediately I could see that it was the Mika sticker. I began to smooth out the crumple further just to make sure. It was so good to touch that sticker once more. In that moment something happened. It began with a tiny tingle in the tip of my finger. The tingle spread to other fingers. It worked its way down my fingers and changed from a tingle into a shock wave which swept over my whole body. I was changing back. Already my hands were no longer Mika's hands but those of a small boy. Soon it would be my arms, legs, and toes. In a few seconds I'd be back to my normal me.

Knocker saw it too.

'Spider,' he shouted. 'Spider, it's you.'

The room was getting bigger and so was Knocker. It was all getting too big for comfort.

No . . . Please . . . Not so soon . . . Let me be Mika for just a bit longer, said a voice in my head.

But it was too late. Before I could stop him he grabbed the sticker out of my hand. Then he ripped it up into tiny pieces and threw them into my face. But he wasn't done yet. He lunged at me with his fist. I ducked just in time.

It was time to make a move. I turned and ran. Being small may have many disadvantages but at least I can move fast when I really need to. My feet touched the top stair and I skipped all the way down them. Up above my head I could hear Knocker lumbering after me. His feet crashed down the stairs. 'Spider . . . Spider,' he shouted.

I ran to the door and leapt outside. I tried to run fast but my feet had grown smaller inside the big wellington boots and my dad's big coat was dragging along the ground. My feet were slipping about and I was slowing down. Then the coat caught on something and I lurched forward and fell to the ground. Knocker could only be a few seconds behind me. I had to think fast. There was no looking back to see how close Knocker was. I pulled my feet out of the boots and my arms out of the coat. Then I ran like I'd never run before. I ran all the way home without stopping and once inside I shut the door tight behind me.

I decided I was through with football. It was too much hassle. Maybe another sport would be safer. The kind of sport where there was no chance of getting trapped into a body that wasn't your own. What about a really boring sport like fishing or dancing? I don't really mind if it is boring as long as it is *safe*.

Even knitting woolly hats seemed appealing so long as the knitting needles didn't get it into their heads to call you a wimp. So that was it then. Football and me were going to be strangers from now on. No football videos or comics. Certainly no stickers. And as for playing football again—well, forget it.

Next day at school I had to go and see Mrs Warren, the headteacher, in her office.

'Come and sit down, Sam,' she said. Then she smiled at me.

'Mr Brailsford came to see me about the football match,' she said. 'I'm very sorry, Sam.'

I looked up at her. Why was she sorry? Was she sorry that the team had drawn when we should have won? Was she sorry that I had picked up the ball and given away a penalty? Why can't adults explain things better?

Perhaps she sensed what was going through my mind.

'I'm sorry about the way Paul Osborn hit you and that you have a black eye,' she said.

'Oh,' I replied.

'We have suspended him from school all week,' she said. 'He won't be coming back until all the bullying is sorted out. I hope you can now relax and enjoy life in school,' she said.

Knocker suspended for a whole week was the best news ever. As for relaxing—well, I don't know about that.

I went back to class in a daze. Charlton offered me some of his sweets. I took three. Ravi said he'd help me with the homework. I gave him my book.

'You can do it for me if you like,' I said.

You never know how long your good luck will last. I went home and tried to watch TV without flicking onto any channels showing football. It was not easy.

My mother's voice called out from downstairs.

'Sam . . . Sam.'

I didn't answer.

'Sam . . . somebody to see you.'

'I'm not in,' I shouted back.

A few minutes later there was a knock on my bedroom door.

'Go away,' I said.

It went quiet and then a small voice said, 'Who said "He can't run, he can't tackle, and he can't head a ball. The only time he goes forward is to toss a coin?" Who said it, Sam?'

'Go away, Tara.'

'It was Tommy Docherty about his captain, Ray Wilkins.'

I said nothing.

'I've come to cheer you up, Sam,' she said.

I still said nothing. Seconds passed. They seemed like hours. Then my bedroom door opened and Tara stepped in.

'How did you get your black eye?' she asked.

I wasn't going to answer that question.

'You got thumped, didn't you? I heard all about it,' she said pulling a football programme out of her pocket.

'I got this for you to look at. I bet you can read it with your good eye. My dad got it. He says he's going to take me to a big Premier match next week . . . and you can come if you like.'

'I've given up football.'

She put the programme into my hands.

'Now you are being daft. You can't give up just like that . . . and anyway that Knocker has been banned.'

'Banned?'

'Yeah. I saw Charlton Harris and he told me.'

I looked at Tara out of my good eye as she sat on a chair near my bedroom window with the sun shining behind her head.

'It all went wrong,' I said.

'What did?' she said.

And I told her. Everything. About the wrong

blazer badge. All about Mika power and the school match. The penalty mix up and me catching the ball. Even getting trapped in Mika's body.

She didn't say anything. She just listened. I thought she might laugh at me when it came to catching the ball. But she didn't. After I'd finished she said, 'It shows one thing, Sam.'

'What?'

'You're a goalie, of course. Not a striker. Never a striker. You should play in goal and then you'll be a really good player.'

I looked at her again. Her voice didn't seem so squeaky now. But more than that I knew she was right.

There was no Knocker at school the next day. His dad had heard about the punch and had taken him up north for a few days to cool him down.

Then it came to the football lesson. Most of the kids just looked at me and said nothing but Charlton said hello. When the two teams were picked I said, 'Can I play in goal, sir?'

'Yes,' said Mr Brailsford with a grin. 'That would be a good idea.'

It was. I had a fair game. Nothing brilliant but I kept a clean sheet and made one decent save. I had no Mika sticker in my pocket and no zap power to call on. But I managed.

That afternoon Charlton Harris came running along the corridor after me.

'Guess what?' he said.

'What?'

'You've been picked again.'

I stared at his ginger-freckled face. Was this some sick joke?

'You've been picked for goalie. Mr Brailsford says you're playing on Wednesday. It's the cup replay.'

I ran along the pavement. I ran past the trees in Lime Grove with their lumbering branches and their outstretched arms ready to trip me up. But I needed to run faster or Goodall's Paper Shop would be closed for the day and then it would be too late. I needed another Mika sticker. If I was going to play again in the school team I had to have the zap power. I couldn't do without it. I knew I could get trapped into Mika's body but I just had to have that sticker.

Into High Street I sprinted just as Mrs Goodall was turning the notice in the window from 'Open' to 'Closed'.

'You've cut it fine,' she said moving off towards the shop counter.

'I ran all the way,' I said trying to get my breath back.

'I can see that,' she said. 'You're all of a lather.'

I didn't know what a lather was but I knew what I had to ask for.

'I was wondering if . . . '

'No,' she said turning off the light above a display cabinet.

'But . . . '

'Sold out.'

She started to take off her referee's black uniform and was ready to hang it on a nail in the wall.

'I need some stickers . . . '

'I said we've sold out. Last lot went ages ago.'

Then she peered closer at me.

'What do you want those for anyway?'

'I . . . I . . . '

'Be snappy,' she said. 'I'm shutting up shop.'

'I want the magic,' I said.

'There's no magic in them,' she said. 'The only real magic you need is in that head of yours.'

'Oh,' I said, not making any sense of what she was saying. Her uniform was hung on the nail and her hand moved towards the light switches for the whole shop. Then it stopped and dipped back into the top pocket of her uniform.

'Still, if it's stickers you want there's just these left,' she said and threw me a small packet just like she had the last time.

'Now take yourself off,' she said. 'I'm ready for my tea.'

Once outside the shop I ripped open the

packet of stickers just like I had last time. But there was something wrong. The first one was blank. It was just a blank white square. So was the second, the third, and the fourth. All white blanks. I turned back towards the shop. The lights were out and the sign said CLOSED in bold print. Mrs Goodall was in the back room having her tea and not even the hammering on the door of a small boy's fists was going to disturb her.

12

There had to be an answer. I turned the stickers over and over in my hands. I held one up towards my bedroom light to see if anything shone through. I peeled off the backing part to see if they'd been printed the wrong way round and put it on again but there wasn't a letter of writing or scrap of a picture on any of them. I even found an old magnifying glass which had come out of a Christmas cracker but even through that the stickers were blank.

I put them on top of my computer desk, turned on the telly and tried to forget about them. But it was like trying to forget you've got chronic toothache or rotten belly ache. Why had Mrs Goodall wanted to give me blank stickers?

I went over to the computer desk and picked one up again. It seemed to have a tiny dot of black on it like a bit of dirt. I rubbed at it with my finger but the black dot didn't move. I opened my mouth and gave the sticker a big huff with my hot breath and just for a second I did see a faint shape on it. I huffed again and again on all the stickers but nothing appeared.

Maybe I'd dreamed it or something but that faint shape was me. What had Mrs Goodall said?

'The real magic is in your head.'

Somehow I'd just have to manage the football match without Mika. But how? If the magic was in my head then what kind of magic was that? Perhaps she was saying I had to make my own magic . . . out there on the pitch. Wow, this was scary.

I had to be ready for anything . . . that was clear. Ready to leap for the ball in that goal. Ready to throw myself forwards . . . to dive low to the left and right. I had to catch or punch the ball clear if I needed to. More than anything I couldn't be a chicken. If a whole pack of forwards was charging for the goal with the ball at their feet I'd have to dive down and grab it

off them. Then and only then could I be a
goalkeeper.

I stood up on my bed and tried to imagine a
mob of footballers charging out of the bathroom
along the landing past Amber's bedroom
heading straight towards me. I got my football
and put it on the spot where I thought it might
be on the pitch. I began to count aloud.

'One . . . two . . . ' knowing that by the time
I got to five I'd have to dive off the bed and get
the ball before the forwards did.

'Three . . . four . . . five.'

I dived off the bed, hit the wall with a crash, and crunched my knees on the floor. Mum came running up the stairs and even Amber came out of her bedroom.

'What's going on?' asked Mum.

'I was playing football.'

My mother stared at me.

'You can't play football in your bedroom dressed in your pyjamas, Sam. Now get to sleep.'

Sleep was one thing I couldn't do. The next half an hour was spent bouncing up and down on my bed punching and catching footballs in my goal as quietly as I could. I tried to think how I could get myself out of the house before my mother got up the next morning.

They are all going to the school game. Tara and her dad will be there to cheer me.

'I'll keep my fingers crossed the whole game,' said Tara. Even Mum and Amber are going to a football match for the very first time.

'Just so long as the match is over by five o'clock,' said Mum. 'It's Amber's dancing class tonight and we can't be late for that.'

Even as I headed for the changing room a big crowd was pouring onto the field for this last match of the season. It was really going to be something very special. I tried not to think about all those people and just looked straight ahead. I was right by the door of the changing room when who should I see but Knocker hanging around. I thought he was still up north with his dad. No such luck.

But I wasn't going to let him spoil this

special day and walked straight past him and into the changing room. Then the rest of our team came in and so did Mr Brailsford. It was time for another of his pep talks, only he took us off to a classroom for this one and went over what we had to do in the game.

I found it hard to listen to what Mr Brailsford was saying. All I wanted to do was to get changed and get the match over and done with. At last we were back in the changing room and putting on the football strip. I reached into my football shorts pocket to find that blank sticker Mrs Goodall had given me. Even though it was blank I needed its luck. Luck is so important in a big game like this. But I couldn't find the sticker at all. I pulled at the pocket. I turned the pocket inside out and still no sticker. I could feel myself going very red in my face. I went through all my pockets and still no sticker. It must be there somewhere. It had to be. Mr Brailsford came into the room.

'What's wrong, Sam?'

'My football sticker has gone, sir.'

'Check your pockets.'

'I have, sir.'

'Then check your bag.'

'It's a special sticker, sir . . . to bring me luck.'

'What kind of a sticker was it?'

'Erm . . . blank, sir.'

'A blank sticker . . . Sam, this is ridiculous. You don't need a blank sticker. Now get ready. The whistle will be going to start the match.'

My head was in a whirl. I couldn't play without that sticker. I just couldn't. Where had it gone? How had it gone? Nobody would want to steal a blank sticker from the changing rooms . . . nobody would do a thing . . . Yes, they would. They would. If it was a banned kid. A big bully kid who was hanging round the changing rooms . . . he would do it.

'Sam . . . Sam . . . get yourself changed. The match is going to start *any minute!*'

Smack! The ball hits the cross bar. I'm nowhere near it. A few centimetres lower and it would have been in the back of the net. I'm still in a whirl. Jelly legs and heart thumping. My legs won't move. I can't move from the spot. I'm no good at all. There might as well be an empty goal for them to shoot at. I can't stop a flea scoring a goal. This is terrib—Look out . . . look out!

The ball bounces off the cross bar and falls straight at the feet of their big number 9. He charges forward. He's bigger than Knocker. Much bigger. He barges one of our defenders out of the way and then a second. Surely that was a foul, ref. A yellow card at least. But there's no foul given, no whistle blown and on he comes towards me. I suddenly realize there's only me between him and the goal.

I want to crawl away. I'm not up to this. I want to step back and out of his way. Way off on the touchline I see Knocker. He's got my blank sticker. Stolen it. I know he has.

I can hear the breath of their number 9. I've got to do something. Come on, Sam. Come on. Don't be a spider. Not now. I take a step forward and another. I have to narrow his shooting angle. The further I step towards him the narrower the angle and the smaller his target. Keep calm . . . stay on your feet . . . and keep your eye on the ball.

Now he makes a move. The ball is close by his feet. He goes to his right. He wants to dribble the ball past me and lob it into an empty net. No way. It's my turn now. I pounce and dive at his feet . . . Steady . . . steady. If you pull him down it will be a penalty. My hands are on the ball. I pull and tug and the ball comes closer to my chest. Grip it tight. Don't let it go. Just don't.

Ouch! His foot hits me in the stomach. I can't breathe. Then his legs buckle and he falls like an elephant right on top of me.

The ref blows his whistle at last.

'Blinding save, Sam,' shouts somebody but I'm too dazed to know who it is. The world is spinning and reeling. All that I know is that I'm clutching the ball and I mean to keep it. The whistle blows again fiercely this time and Mr Brailsford is running onto the pitch carrying a bag.

'Steady, Sam,' he says and sits me down on the pitch. 'Easy now.' He gives me a drink and looks into my eyes.

'How do you feel?'

'OK.'

Then he takes a cold sponge from his bag and squeezes a load of water down my neck. I start to shiver and he says, 'I think you should go off for a bit. Have a rest.'

'No.'

'But you're shivering.'

'That water was freezing. Let me carry on.'

A few minutes later and I'm back on my feet and back in goal. Charlton takes the goal kick for me and wellies it right down to the far side of the pitch. I take a few deep breaths and the world stops spinning and wobbling about. Then the whistle goes for half time and it's still nil–nil.

Soon after the start of the second half the big number 9 tries a shot at goal again from some distance out. It's a volley right on target and I don't see it until it's right up on me. I'm diving to the left and the ball is going to my right. I try to change direction but it's no good. Somehow the ball strikes the heel of my boot and squirts off across the goal line. If any of their players had been on the spot it would have been a certain goal.

As it is Charlton is there to whack it out for a corner. The goal area is so bunched up I can't see anything.

'Give me some space,' I shout but nobody is listening because the corner kick has already been taken. The ball is zooming towards the goal. It's soaring and lifting right towards the net. I shall have to leap for it. I know I will. Don't jump too soon or you'll miss it by a mile. Steady . . . *now* . . . leap for it *now*. I'm straining my arms and back . . . Somehow I catch the ball. It sticks in both hands firm and true.

'Sam . . . Sam . . . ' shouts Charlton on the wing.

Now is our chance. If I can pass it out to him quick enough we can break from defence to attack in an instant. Yet the pass has to be right to his feet. Only then will the break be on. A kick's no good. I'm no good at kicking. The ball is in my hand and Charlton in my sights. Overarm. It will have to be an overarm throw.

The ball is on its way. It lands right by his feet and Charlton is flying. Yes, he's flying down the wing in masses of space. He clears one defender and then a second. Ryan is in the centre.

'Pass it, Charlton . . . please . . . please pass it,' I scream. But I'm too far away. My voice is lost in the length of the pitch. I can't watch and close my eyes.

'Yeees . . . Goooaall!'

The pass was made and Ryan has scored.

'Goooaall . . . Goooaall!' our chant echoes round the ground. But Mr Brailsford is shouting even louder.

'Concentrate now . . . don't give it away.'

I jolt back to my senses. The few minutes after you've scored a goal is the most likely time you'll give one away. You become sloppy. Inside my gloves I grip my hands tight and jog up and down on my toes.

Somehow we hang on in there. It's still one–nil with just a few minutes to go. Their number 9 has the ball and is heading upfield. I've got him covered. My eyes are on him all the time. As he reaches the edge of the penalty area Josh charges at him and with a huge swathing kick knocks him clean off his feet.

PENALTY! PENALTY! shout the opposition in a loud chorus. The ref blows his whistle with a shrill blast. Josh is given a yellow card and they are given a penalty.

For the first time in the match my hand goes to my pocket. To the place where the sticker of Mika used to be. There's no pocket there now and certainly no sticker.

Now surely the opposition will score and save the match. Our first victory will be no more than a lost dream. Number 9, the team's captain, steps forward and places the ball on the spot. Everyone is quiet now. Out on the touchline Mum and Amber are quiet and so is Tara. Even Knocker is silent. All the players stand still. Number 9 too stands still. He looks at the ball then at the goal and then back at the ball again. He shakes his hands by his sides and then takes three very deliberate steps back. All eyes are on the ball now . . .

Please, Mika, come to my rescue.

He runs forward swiftly and hits the ball hard and true.

Remember the only real magic you need is in your own head.

The ball is right on target and zooms towards the bottom corner of the net. It is perfection. Yet a blurred low shape is moving to the same spot too. A small blurred shape in green is hurling itself towards the ball. Arms fling forward and in a rolling mass of ball and gloves and goalkeeper's body the penalty is saved. The ref blows the final whistle and the under 13s have gained their first victory.

One small goalkeeper is lifted aloft amongst cheers which echo round the ground. Everybody gathers round him. One big boy, once a bully just back from school suspension, stands alone and then walks away by himself.

There's Only One Danny Ogle

Helena Pielichaty

Illustrated by Glyn Goodwin

ACKNOWLEDGEMENTS

for Pete, Jurek, Vytas, Big Dave and all who sit in the John Smith Stand, as well as to Nick and Aaron in the posh end, for their timeless comments on the beautiful game.

I would also like to thank Steve Lee and John Wolfenden for helping me in my research about youth teams and junior football.

This book is dedicated to David Moulds, even if he does support Leicester City, for his support and encouragement.

1

Hi, my name is Danny Ogle and my life is over. Want to know why? We've moved to the countryside. Any old mates who want to find me can contact me at:

Danny Ogle
Dump Cottage
Dead Boring Lane
Little to Do
Middle of Nowhere
England

No offence if you like living in a village. Cows and fields and fresh air are fine if you like that kind of thing but I'm a town boy. I was born in a town, grew up in a town, and support a football team with 'town' in its name.

A few months ago, when Mum said we were moving somewhere better, what I thought she meant was:

◉ My bedroom window would overlook the McAlpine Stadium
◉ We'd have Sky TV
◉ The garden would be big enough for five-a-side matches
◉ McDonald's would be across the road
◉ I wouldn't have to change schools so I could try out for the A team.

What she really meant was:

◉ My bedroom window overlooked miles and miles of *nothing*
◉ We'd have ordinary TV but sky was available if I looked outside (ha ha)

◎The garden was big enough for a football pitch but I'd have to get rid of the orchard first

◎Forget McDonald's. All we had was one piddly shop run by someone called Mrs Dobb

◎But worst of all, not only did I have to change schools, I had to change counties.

Like I said, my life is over.

2

It was Gran who helped me to see things differently. Gran's an auxiliary nurse at the hospital. She once did our ace defender Kevin Green's bedpans when he had a broken leg; she's *that* famous.

Last night we had our usual conversation. It went something like this:

On the Phone

Gran: Hello, love. Have you finished unpacking yet?

Me: Sort of.

Gran: Your mum says the cottage is lovely.

Me: It's all right.

Gran: It's a pity you're only renting it. Where is it the owners live? Dubai?

Me: Something like that.

Gran: Hey! You start your new school next week, don't you? What's it called again?

Me: (dead grumpy) Westhorpe Primary School for Turnips.

Gran: (sighs patiently) Come on, Danny, change the record. Think positive.

Me: How can I? I won't know one person there except Karla and sisters don't count. I hate change.

Gran: I thought you wanted to be a professional footballer when you grow up?

Me: I do!

Gran: Well, what about when you're transferred? You'll need to move from one end of the country to the other every few seasons then.

Me: I guess.

Gran: Have you found out about Westhorpe's football team yet?

Me: No.

Gran: Your mum was telling me there's under thirty pupils. I bet you get straight into the 'A' team—they might even make you captain, a lad with your talent and experience.

Now that gave me something to think about. No matter how much I tried at my old school the coach always stuck me in the 'B' squad. It wasn't because I wasn't good enough for the 'A' lot, you understand, it was just that we were an outstanding year with hundreds to choose from. Plus coach wanted someone decent in the 'B's so they wouldn't lose heart. I was sacrificed, actually.

Inspired, I handed over the phone to Mum and dashed outside to practise my ball juggling. There was no point allowing my skills to erode. A captain has to set a good example.

As soon as Mum had finished on the phone I asked her where the school handbook was. 'The one you said you'd rather support United than read?' she teased.

'That's the one.'

'Next to the microwave.'

'Thanks, chuck,' I said, jogging into the kitchen.

She followed me, grinning, obviously delighted to have her old son back again. 'Looking for something in particular?' she asked.

'Team details,' I replied, flicking through the pages. 'School uniform—not interested—school dinners—no way—school rules—not bothered—job vacancies—who cares? I can't find anything about the football teams,' I said in disgust. 'At Frank Worthington's there were tons.'

'Let me have a look,' Mum said. 'Hmm . . . could this be it?' She pointed a fingernail at something called 'After School Activities'.

Together we scanned the columns.

Westhorpe School After School Activities

3.30 p.m. to 5.00 p.m. daily. Come to as many as you like. Tuck shop every day.

Choose from:

Mondays	Chess Club
Tuesdays	Country Dancing
Wednesdays	Gardening Club
Thursdays	Computer Club
Fridays	Westhorpe Wanderers

'Do you think that's the name of the football team?' I asked doubtfully, staring at Friday.

'The Westhorpe Wanderers? Like Bolton Wanderers? Could be,' Mum agreed.

'It's got to be, hasn't it? There's nothing else near. I wonder who takes it? There's no names.'

'You'll find out soon enough. Have you seen this?'

'What?'

Mum turned over to the last page in the handbook. The page was blank apart from a heading inviting new pupils to write about themselves. She had mentioned it a dozen times before but I'd 'forgotten' about it. I hated writing—especially about myself. 'Do I have to?' I whinged.

'It's up to you,' she shrugged, 'but why miss a chance to impress them? If nothing comes on the market we're going to be here until Christmas at least—that must be enough time for a few matches. You could make out you're on the transfer list and they're lucky to have you.'

'They are lucky to have me!' I agreed. 'Got a pen?'

4

Mrs Bulinski, my new Head as well as class teacher, was a stocky woman with dark hair and square red glasses. Karla, who was going through a reading-nothing-but-Roald Dahl phase, stared at her and whispered nervously, 'She looks like *Miss Trunchbull*.'

I was thinking the same thing but I was too busy trying to look keen and captain-ish to whisper back. The Head beamed at us both before addressing the school and suddenly she didn't look like Miss Trunchbull at all—she looked kind and friendly. 'Well, everybody, welcome back to a new year at Westhorpe. Did you all have a good holiday?' There was much nodding and 'yer-ing' from the kids around me on the carpet. They seemed cool enough. One boy, a kid called Curtis, had already said I could join his mates at break. I began to relax.

Mrs Bulinski beamed again. 'Good. Firstly, let me introduce you to Mrs Speed. Mrs Speed is on supply until we get a new teacher.' Eyes turned to the side of the classroom where a tall, spindly woman with grey hair nodded and smiled from behind the piano. I tried to guess which one coached The Wanderers. Neither looked exactly sporty but that meant nothing. There had been a dead fat kid called Martin Mallinson at my old school who could outrun the lot of us.

Mrs Bulinski switched her attention to Karla and me. 'And we're very pleased to have two new pupils starting today as well; Danny, a Year Five and Karla, a Year Three.'

I felt everyone staring at me so I focused on

my new trainers. 'Would one of you like to tell us a bit about yourselves?'

Karla shook her head, even though I knew she had spent ages on her introduction. Realizing she was even more nervous than I was, I gave her a 'don't worry' dig and stood up. Pulling the sheet from out of my pocket, I cleared my throat, and began to read:

A little bit about me
(for new pupils only)

Hi, my name is Danny Ogle and I'm nine and a half—I'll be ten in February. I live with my mum, Debbie, her partner Steve, and my sister, Karla. Steve is a photographer and Mum is a nursery nurse. My dad lives in Germany. I don't see him much. I'll let Karla tell you about herself.

I'm the odd one out in my family because I'm football mad. The only other person who likes it is my gran, though my grandad did, too, when he was alive. My gran takes me to see all Town's home matches when she can. Town's the name of the team I support. I've supported them since I was 6. I have two dreams: one is to be chosen as a mascot and run on the pitch at the McAlpine Stadium. The second is to be selected for Town's Centre of Excellence. Kevin Green is my favourite player because he's hard and gets stuck in.

I love playing football, as well as watching it. I like mid-field or attack but I'm very versatile. My coach said I was good at finding space and ball control. Most important is that I am not a ball-hog or a goal-hanger.

I am never late for practices and am available for any home or away fixtures. I don't mind taking the kit home to wash but we only have one car and Steve uses that a lot for his work so I might need a lift to away games. I look forward to joining the Westhorpe Wanderers and promise to help bring back a trophy or two this season.

Someone laughed just then and put me off. Mrs Bulinski cleaned her glasses with the edge of her skirt and gave the culprit a deadeye at the same time. 'That was very good, Danny, well done, but I think you've got hold of the wrong end of the stick. Spencer Mason, as you found Dan's mistake so amusing perhaps you'll have the good manners to explain to him what the Westhorpe Wanderers do.'

This Spencer kid stared dumbly into space. 'They wander around Westhorpe,' he said in a bored voice.

'Wondering why they bother!' added a comedian next to him.

Mrs Bulinski held up a warning finger and they shut up. 'The Westhorpe Wanderers go on walks and find out all sorts about nature, Danny. I'm afraid they've got nothing to do with football.'

'When's football practice then?' I asked.

'It isn't, I'm afraid. We don't have a team here.'

'You can always try country dancing!' the Spencer kid shouted out dead sarky.

'Lend me one of your skirts then!' I fired back. Loads of kids laughed but Spencer and his mate stared sourly into my face.

Great.

'Give this to *them* when we get in,' I ordered Karla at the end of school. I thrust a note into her hand and hurried along Low Street.

At home I ran upstairs before either Mum or Steve had a chance to start grilling me. I heard Mum ask Karla what the matter was but I banged the bedroom door shut before I could hear her reply.

A few minutes later Mum tapped on the door and entered. 'What's this mean?' she asked softly. She read out my note:

1.	No I didn't
2.	Sausage casserole, lumps of mash, iced bun
3.	No one

I sighed heavily. 'It's the answer to the questions you always ask when I come in from school.'

'Ah. I see. So, one, you didn't have a nice day, two, you had sausage casserole for lunch and three, you sat by yourself.'

'That's about the size of it,' I mumbled.

'Karla told me about the football team.'

'Huh!'

'I'm sorry, Danny.'

I just stared at the wall. Mum and Steve didn't really understand about football so I couldn't tell her how I felt. How nothing gives me that tingly feeling in the pit of my stomach like when I'm running onto the pitch at the start of a match with the team, getting into position and waiting for the whistle to blow. And how nothing *in this universe* compares to scoring a goal. *Nothing*. Without any of that, school would be torture.

'It's early days yet, love,' Mum said, 'and if we don't find a house to buy that we like in Westhorpe we might look in one of the bigger villages and the first thing we'll check out is whether the school has a football team.'

'Promise?'

'Promise.'

I felt better already. My mum always keeps her promises.

Meanwhile, I took Gran's advice and made the most of things. I kept my head down and listened in class, answered a few questions now and again and even joined in with singing hymns during assembly. I had to wait until Friday last thing, though, for Games.

Mrs Bulinski emerged from the office in her ordinary clothes, the whistle dangling round her neck the only clue to what was next. I didn't care. At last we were going to have a decent lesson. I was ready in a flash and asked if I could help put out the equipment. 'Equipment? Oh, yes, maybe,' she said, peering through the window. 'I don't like the look of those clouds.'

'Here we go,' Curtis muttered.

I glanced out. There was one tiny cloud about seven hundred miles away. 'Oh, that's nothing,' I said, 'we used to play in hailstones in Yorkshire.'

Mrs Bulinski shuddered. 'Perish the thought,' she said and dispatched Curtis and me to the shed.

I waited impatiently for him to open the door. 'What are we getting out then?' I asked eagerly. 'Cones? Nets? How many balls do we need?'

'Whatever,' Curtis said, standing back to let me go in first.

It was the crummiest games cupboard I'd ever seen. Plastic hoops had been left scattered amongst tangled skipping ropes and soggy beanbags. A rusty netball post lay sideways across like a tree struck by lightning. Then, in a far corner, I saw it. I let out a low gasp of horror and stumbled forward.

'What's up?' Curtis asked in alarm. 'Have you found Mrs Dobb's missing cat? Is it dead? Don't show me if it is—I'll puke.'

'Worse. Look.'

I held out the sad leather ball cradled in my arms. It had been good quality once but was now dirty and deflated, its whole side caved in like a baseball glove. 'That's criminal, that is,' I said.

'Get used to it, mate,' Curtis replied, 'Mrs B hates PE.'

Before I had time to have a heart attack, Alfie Cruickshank, a Year Four, came belting round the corner. 'You've to come back in—we're doing mat work.'

'See what I mean?' Curtis shrugged, locking up again.

'You mean this is normal?'

He nodded. 'She does it every lesson. By the time we've got the mats out we'll have done three arms stretches and a forward roll and that'll be it. Like I said, get used to it.'

'Used to it? Used to no PE?'

'Yeah. We don't even bother bringing kit in any more, except for swimming on Wednesdays.'

My life was *so* over.

7

I couldn't wait to get home. I was going to pack straightaway then phone AA Roadwatch for the route back to Gran's. If Mum refused to take me I'd walk the whole one hundred and four miles. One thing was certain. There was *no way* I was staying at Westhorpe Primary.

That was until Mrs Bulinski dropped her bombshell just before half three. 'I've been mulling over Danny's speech yesterday,' she began, 'and it got me thinking. We have never been a very sporty school, but I do hate seeing enthusiasm like Danny's go to waste, and I know he's not the only one. Now, it's no secret that I don't know one end of a football court from another but if any Year Fours, Fives, or Sixes are interested I'm willing to organize some sort of football practice. *Is* anyone interested?'

My arm shot up faster than a rocket. Five or six others joined me. 'Oh,' Mrs B said, surprised. 'OK. Now keep your hand up if you know any grown-up who'd like to train you.' Every hand fell, including mine. I knew neither Mum nor Steve had time. 'Hmm, just as I thought. Never mind, I'll send a note home but if no one volunteers by the end of next week we'll have to think again. Meanwhile, I'll put a notice on the board for you to sign up. Fewer than ten and it won't be worth it,' she warned.

I belted home. 'Turkey dinosaurs, chips, and cornflake tart!' I gasped, adding quickly, 'Which one of you wants to coach football?'

'Football? What's that?' Mum teased, then said no, like I knew she would.

'Can't, Dan. I never know where I'll be one day from the next with work,' Steve said, like I knew he would.

It was the same with Curtis and Alfie when they called round. Alfie's parents both worked and Curtis's mum had just had a baby. 'Someone'll do it,' I said, trying to be optimistic.

'I want to know why Mrs B's suddenly starting a team. She's always said no before,' Curtis said.

Alfie answered: 'Oh, that's simple. Remember the Huckerby twins left to go to Tuxton because they wanted to do more sport?'

'Yeah.'

'My mum's a governor and I heard her telling Dad Mrs B's panicking in case Oggy goes, too. We've got an inspection next term and the school might close if we don't get numbers up.'

'Where's Tuxton?' I asked.

'It's another village school like ours except a bit bigger and they win loads of tournaments.'

'I wanna go to Tuxton!' I said, pretending to cry.

'No you don't. Their Head Mr Girton's really mean and strict. Mrs Bulinski's miles better.'

There was nothing wrong with 'strict' in my book, as long as people were fair with it. Still, you couldn't tell that to kids who weren't used to the sporting mentality so I just shrugged and led the way round the side of the house. 'Come on, let's have a kick about,' I said. I chalked the outline of a goal mouth against the gable end and we took turns, two on one, tackling and shooting.

Curtis had been to a football summer school over in Lincoln, so he was pretty good. He got

the ball off me nearly every time. 'I thought country kids couldn't play,' I grumbled.

'Think again, town boy!' he yelled, belting the ball against the brickwork.

Alfie had never played in his life and it showed. His toe-ender kicks were all over the place and he shouted 'Help me, Mummy!' as a joke if anyone tried to tackle him. Then he missed the ball completely and fell onto the road. We took him inside and Steve cleaned him up.

'We need a proper pitch to play on,' I said, 'why don't we go down to the school field?'

The school field was across a small side road opposite the school. It had full-sized goalposts but I hadn't been able to suss out the state of the grass because the field gate was always padlocked. Curtis told me why. 'It's out of bounds except during lessons; the caretaker has to protect his onions,' he explained.

'Do what?'

'Protect his onions. Mr Spanner grows vegetables round the edges of the field.'

'Never! How come?'

'I think the field used to be bigger and years ago Westhorpe pupils used to grow things on it but then they stopped and the council sold part of it for housing.'

'The Lawns Estate,' Alfie informed us

through clenched teeth, as Steve dabbed a little too hard.

Curtis nodded then continued. 'Mr Spanner had to move the vegetable patches closer and I think they've kind of accidentally-on-purpose spread since Mrs Bulinski came because she hardly uses it. He's got clematis growing up the goalposts if you look closely.'

'Now I've heard everything,' I said in amazement.

Alfie was picking shale out of his bony kneecap. 'We can practise in my garden until we find somewhere else,' he offered.

'Is it big enough?' I asked.

'Oh, I think you'll find it adequate.'

'Cool. How about Friday?'

'Right-ho.'

I couldn't wait to check out the list at school but by Friday only six genuine names had appeared and I wished two of those weren't there. Shelby was all right but Spencer Mason and Troy Hallett, both Year Sixes, thought they were 'it'.

School Football Team

Sign below:

Curtis Lamb
Alfie Cruickshank
Danny Ogle
David Beckham
Emile Heskey
Michael Owen
Shelby Newton
Troy Hallett (the best)
Spencer Mason (king)
Homer Simpson
Al COHOLIC

'Is that the lot? Six poxy names?' I said. Alfie pointed out that *was* nearly half the juniors. 'And no parent's volunteered to take us yet,' I moaned.

'Don't be down-hearted, chaps. Football practice at my house tonight, Shelby's coming too,' Alfie reminded us.

Well, it was *something* I supposed.

9

'This is your garden?' I gawped. Curtis and Shelby laughed. They'd both been here before.

'Told you it was adequate,' Alfie said. His lawn was so huge you could hardly see Westhorpe Hall, the massive house where Alfie lived, at the other end.

'You must be loaded,' I said.

'Of course,' Alfie replied matter-of-factly. 'Now can we get on with the football? I want you to teach me how to kick properly. I thought we could use Justin and Justout as goalposts.' He pointed to two naked stone cherubs a few metres apart.

'You're the boss.'

For half an hour Curtis and I took it in turns to show Alfie how to use different parts of his foot to pass and kick accurately. He *sort of* got the hang of it but kept trying to kick the ball as soon as it came to him without taming it first. Shelby, who had an older sister who played at secondary, was quite skilled. She had a strong left foot but got flustered if the ball didn't go exactly where she wanted it. 'I'm fed up of this. I'll go in goal,' she said.

'May I take a penalty like they do on TV?' Alfie begged.

'Sure,' we said, and stood back.

He rolled up his sleeves, licked his lips, ran, and kicked. Whack! The ball went straight into Justout's chubby belly and bounced off again into the distance.  'You've knocked his tinky-winky off!' Shelby shrieked.

'Help me look for it,' Alfie called, but we were too busy killing ourselves laughing.

None of us noticed the kid until he stepped out from behind the bushes. 'Do you want this?' he asked, holding the football.

'No, we want this,' Alfie grinned, holding up the stone willy. 'Who are you?'

The kid shrugged. He was about our age, with long straggly hair dotted with coloured beads. 'I'm Devlin. My da's up at the house, asking if we can camp in your wood for a while.'

'Oh, OK,' Alfie said. He turned to us. 'Mother won't mind, she never does.'

'Can I join yous?' Devlin asked.

'Certainly,' Alfie agreed. 'You and I'll take Curtis and Danny. Shelby, are you OK in goal still?' Shelby nodded.

It was much better with five of us. I started off with possession and crossed it to Curtis, then ran forward. Alfie tried to tackle Curtis but he was too slow and Curtis dodged him easily, crossing back to me. Suddenly, Devlin arrived out of nowhere, trapped the ball deftly with his right, positioned himself, then shot forward with his left and fired. Shelby stood no chance. Nobody would have.

A shiver ran down my back. I'd seen enough magic players to know Devlin was one. 'Will you be going to school while you're here?' I asked. Devlin pulled a sour face and nodded.

'Seven!' we chorused.

'Same time, same place Monday?' Alfie suggested.

10

Devlin arrived late on Monday morning, looking uncomfortable. Spencer hissed in a low voice: 'Nose pegs, everybody, the gyppos have landed.'

I told him to bog off and made room for Devlin next to me.

At break, he signed up for the team. 'Can we still go ahead with only seven?' we asked Mrs Bulinski in the playground.

'We'll see,' she said. We all know what that means in teacher-speak. Desperate, I put up my own notice next to hers:

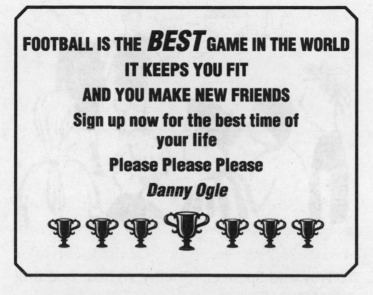

FOOTBALL IS THE *BEST* GAME IN THE WORLD
IT KEEPS YOU FIT
AND YOU MAKE NEW FRIENDS
Sign up now for the best time of
your life
Please Please Please
Danny Ogle

At least I was playing *some* football, though. We met at Alfie's again and played in pairs with one of us taking it in turns in goal. Devlin was so good we soon learned that if we wanted a sniff of the ball we had to be on his side.

'Who coached you?' I asked when we stopped for a break.

'Nobody.'

'Well then, we can tell Mrs B we want nobody to coach us, too. That'll solve a problem!' Alfie joked, then groaned.

'What?' Curtis asked.

'Troy and Spencer,' Shelby sighed, nodding
in the distance.

The two Year Sixes approached, swaggering.
They were both wearing flashy replica kits of
London Premiership teams. Troy had 'keepers
gloves on. 'We thought we'd better turn up for
practice seeing you *forgot* to invite us,' he said.

I hoped Alfie would tell them where to go
but he just shrugged. 'I suppose we should play
as a team,' he said.

'I'm in goal,' Troy declared, taking over.

'Shelby is in goal,' I pointed out.

'*Was* in goal, Yorkshire Pudding, *was* in

goal.' He strolled over and stood between Justin and Justout.

OK, Mason, I thought, let's see what you're made of. 'Alfie was just going to take a penalty,' I said.

'Was I?' Alfie asked.

'Yeah,' I reminded him, 'just like the one you took yesterday.'

His eyes lit up. 'Oh, yes, of course I was.'

'Aim for Justin,' I whispered, knowing he'd miss.

He rolled up his sleeves, licked his lips, ran, and kicked. Whack! Troy went down like a ton of bricks, rolling about and clutching his rude bits in his posh gloves. We all let out a sympathetic 'ooh!'

'I'll go back in goal for a while, shall I?' Shelby suggested.

'OK,' Troy squeaked.

They were all right after that, especially when they realized we might be younger but we were just as good. Neither of them played with much style but they were solid enough. Devlin, of course, was brilliant. 'Not bad for a gyppo,' Spencer admitted at the end. I could tell from the thunderous look on Devlin's face the name-calling wouldn't be lasting much longer and I pitied Spencer and Troy the day they pushed him too far.

But it was a start and I went home happy.

11

The trouble was, having a kick about with just seven of us lost its appeal after a while. Alfie's garden was big but it was still a garden which meant we spent half the time searching for the ball in the rhododendrons and half the time covering Justin and Justout's jangly-danglies with cycle helmets. It was mucking-about-in-the-park stuff. We had to work on Mrs Bulinski—quick.

The next time it was her break duty, Curtis, Alfie, and me followed her round the playground, pleading for a proper practice schedule after school, even though we only had seven people, not the ten she had stipulated.

Mrs Bulinski pushed her glasses up the bridge of her nose and sighed hard. 'All right,' she said, 'if it's so important to you, you can stay behind on Wednesdays and I'll ask someone else to do Gardening Club.'

Alfie immediately grabbed her hand and shook it. 'You really do set a magnificent example to the teaching profession, Mrs Bulinski. You should have a shopping centre named after you,' he stated, just a bit over the top. I mean, a statue would do.

Mrs Bulinski patted him on the shoulder. 'Thank you, Alfie, that's a very nice thought. Now, which one of you is going to break the news to Mr Spanner? He should be at home now if you want to pop round.'

There were groans from the other two. Alfie sounded as if his appendix had just burst. 'Can't you do it, miss?' Curtis said pitifully.

'No.'

'I can't go; I'm too young to die,' Alfie moaned.

'Blimey,' I said, heading for the gate, 'I'll go on my own. It's no wonder we haven't won the World Cup since 1966 with this attitude!'

'He was a good friend, that Danny Ogle,' Alfie sniffed sadly.

I only knew Mr Spanner by sight but he had a fierce reputation. He didn't talk, he barked, and then only one word at a time, such as 'litter!' or 'gate!' Even Hallett and Mason obeyed him immediately, which is more than they did for Mrs Bulinski sometimes.

I wasn't scared of him though. It had nothing to do with being new and not knowing any better. I had an advantage. Confidently, I knocked on his door and delivered the news.

Ten minutes later I was back in class. 'He's alive! Praise the Lord!' Alfie shouted.

'What happened?' Curtis asked.

'We start tomorrow, 3.30 sharp.'

'You're joking! Didn't he go on about his precious vegetables?'

'They did "crop up" during negotiations,' I said wittily.

'And we're still allowed on?'

' 'Course,' I shrugged.

'How did you manage that?'

'I speak fluent caretaker-ish,' I said mysteriously.

Mum laughed when I told her about what I'd done. 'Aww, love. Didn't you tell them about your grandad?'

'I did afterwards.'

'Forty-six years as a school caretaker. He'd seen it all.'

Grandad died when I was seven but I remembered enough about him to handle Mr Spanner. Nasty weather on the field and nasty surprises down the bogs were the two things grandad hated most about the job. All I had to say to Mr Spanner was that I knew, I understood, I sympathized. I wouldn't say I won him over totally, but we each knew where we were coming from. I even wrote a list, with Mum's help, for his approval which I handed to him before the pitch inspection the next day.

TERMS AND AGREEMENTS

The team:

- ◎ No team member will trail back into school in muddy boots.
- ◎ No team member will trespass anywhere near the vegetable patches and flower beds.
- ◎ If a ball strays into one of the patches, it will be retrieved only with permission.
- ◎ We will look after all our equipment ourselves.
- ◎ We will not lose the key to the shed door or be forever asking where it is.

Mr Spanner:

- ◎ Will keep the football pitch in immaculate condition.
- ◎ Will arrange for lines to be painted before important matches.
- ◎ Will stop stray dogs from pooping on the pitch.
- ◎ Will put his clematis somewhere else.

Signed:

D. Ogle for the team

Mr Spanner furrowed his thick grey eyebrows and went 'Hmph'. Which in caretaker-ish means 'agreed'. He then made us follow him round the edges of the field. We marched after him, in single file, as he pointed out areas we had to avoid on pain of death.

Eventually, Mrs Bulinski bustled across so we could start and Mr Spanner returned to school to begin his bin-emptying and toilet flushing. 'Right, are we set?' Mrs B asked.

We were in-deedy.

'And I see you've got all your equipment ready; that's excellent.'

I guess with not being sporty she would class four plastic cones and my leather ball from home as 'equipment' but never mind. She appeared to have brought her own equipment, too; a huge pile of paperwork, her mobile phone, and her chair. As she plonked herself down and opened a buff folder with the words 'numeracy and literacy policies' typed across it, I realized Mrs Bulinski had no intention of even pretending to coach us, she was just there to cover herself in case of accidents. Oh well.

I led us into the centre of the pitch. 'Shall I show you some of the warm-ups and drills we used to do at my old school?' I suggested. We hadn't really bothered at Alfie's but I knew how important they were. Trouble was, I couldn't convince anyone else. They ran round the pitch a couple of times and copied my muscle stretches but when I mentioned cone work they all looked at me blankly and said 'nah!'

'We just want to get on with it,' Troy said, sliding on his 'keeper's gloves and heading for the goalposts. It so annoyed me the way he thought he had a divine right to go in goal just because he had gloves. He wasn't even that good unless the ball came straight at him. Make him stretch either way and he was beaten every time, the plank.

Shelby was much better; she played a lot of basketball at home with her older sister and did karate so she was used to leaping about in all directions but she wouldn't say anything to Troy. The two Year Sixes thought they ruled.

It went OK, though. The ground was a bit bumpy in places but safe enough. It was good to get that feeling of a regular shaped playing area, even though we were only using half the pitch. Alfie's kicks were still the wildest and most unpredictable—an opposition's dream. Only Devlin's speed saved the dahlias from instant splattering time and time again. 'It's not fair! I aim one way and it goes the other. It looks so easy on TV!' Alfie grumbled, getting more and more flustered and upset. 'Why can't I do it?'

Poor Alfie.

Then something strange happened. Mr Spanner, who must have finished his bin emptying and toilet flushing in the fastest

time ever, suddenly reappeared. He stood by the wing and scowled. That wasn't the strange bit. The strange bit was that for the last twenty minutes of practice hardly one of Alfie's shots went out of touch. Every time the ball looked in danger of escaping Mr Spanner would bellow: 'carrots! carrots!' or 'kale! kale!' and look so fierce that Alfie somehow managed to bring the ball under control and whack it desperately away to safety. We made him man of the match.

'Is that it?' Mrs Bulinski asked, looking up in surprise as we trudged past her.

'That's it,' I told her. 'Unless you'll let us stay on longer,' I added hopefully.

'Not today, I'm afraid, Danny, not today.'

I knew from her expression she hadn't watched any of the match but I tried not to mind. She had given up her time to be with us, which is more than anyone else had.

13

Shelby brought her best friend, Alyce Laverack, the following week. 'I'm fed up of being the only girl so I've made her come,' Shelby explained, before adding in a loud whisper, 'Plus she fancies you.'

'I do not!' Alyce protested, going red and elbowing Shelby in the ribs.

'Three times round the field,' I sighed, leading the jog. Great. That was all I needed—love stuff. She'd better not mess about being all girlie or she could get lost.

I think Shelby's teasing had annoyed her, though, because Alyce didn't mess about at all. At first, she seemed really nervous, not even attempting to go for the ball but after we tapped it to her a few times, she got stuck in. Mr Spanner only shouted 'cabbages! cabbages!' at her once which caught her off-guard but she soon got used to the bellowing. She was quite nippy, too, though nothing like Devlin. Devlin was the star but Alyce Laverack would do.

'You were good,' I said to her. 'Will you come next week?'

'If you want me to.'

'Ooooh! "If you want me to!"' Troy mocked as he passed.

'Where are you going?' I said, ignoring his comment.

'What's it to do with you? We've finished, haven't we, *sir*.'

'It's yours and Spencer's turn to put the equipment away,' I pointed out.

'Like that's going to happen!' he said, unstrapping his keeper's gloves before spitting hard into the grass. He and Spencer spent a lot of time spitting—I reckon they think it makes them look professional.

'We're only talking about a few lousy cones,' I pointed out.

'Exactly,' he sneered and walked off with his sidekick.

'It's OK, I'll do it,' Alfie said, running back across the field.

'We should all do it,' I complained. Those two were really starting to get up my nose.

14

It was Monday lunchtime. Devlin and I had to sit on Troy and Spencer's table, worse luck. Spencer began dishing out the shepherd's pie. Somehow he always ended up as server at dinner times, just as Troy always ended up as goalie during practices.

'Is that enough for you, Devlin?' Spencer asked in a dead clever voice as he served Devlin's portion. 'We know how hungry you must be, living in a *caravan*.' He also knew as well as everyone else that Devlin was a vegetarian and had a special meal made for him.

Devlin pushed his plate away. 'I don't eat meat,' he said testily.

'Go hungry, then,' Troy retorted, sliding the plate to a Year Two girl across from him.

Devlin was a weird kid. He could have

smacked either of them with one arm tied behind his back but he never did, no matter what they said to him. I knew Devlin would just have sat there, starving, if nobody did anything, so I put my hand up. 'Yes, Danny?' the dinner assistant, Mrs Howells, asked.

'Have you got Devlin's dinner, miss?'

'Of course I've got his dinner. One of the servers should have collected it.' She fetched the separate meal and placed it in front of Devlin, telling Spencer and Troy off for not doing their job properly.

They homed in on me straight away.

'See your lot got thrashed again,' Troy mocked. Town had gone down two–one on Saturday. Not that I'd been allowed to listen to the highlights on the radio. Oh no. I'd had to go round three poxy houses which were for sale on The Lawns. And we couldn't have morning appointments, could we? Oh no. We could only be fitted in between three and five. Estate agents were obviously not into football. They weren't into finding us anywhere decent either. Every house had been awful—all modern and

no character. Mum had got stressed because time was running out on the cottage and Karla had started crying, saying she liked the cottage and why couldn't we buy that and Steve had snapped at her so I'd shouted, 'Don't yell at her, you're not our dad.' We all ended up walking back to Low Street in silence. Mum had forced me to listen to one of those long, embarrassing chats about Steve not wanting to replace my dad and all that kind of stuff. I hated those—they made me squirm, even though I knew she was right. Finally I'd gone upstairs to phone Gran for a match report only to find we'd been disallowed a penalty in the eighty-ninth minute. All-in-all I was not in the mood for one of Hallett's get-at-the-new-kid sessions.

'We're fifth in the league,' I pointed out to him.

'Yeah, for how long?'

Spencer added his two-pennyworth. 'I don't know why you bother supporting a lame team like that, anyway.'

I could feel my face glowing. Nobody supported Town at Westhorpe—it wasn't local enough and it wasn't one of the glory teams that kids like guess-who followed, either. 'Well, I bet you've never even been to London to see yours play,' I retorted.

Troy splattered baked beans next to my pie. 'Who needs to? They're always on TV because they're the best.'

'You should be supporting your local side like City or County,' I persisted.

'We will when they're top of the Premiership.'

'Fickle,' I said angrily. Glory supporters really did my head in.

'What did you call us?' Spencer asked, shoving his face dangerously close to mine. I could feel the atmosphere around our table change as everyone waited for my reaction.

I backed off. I didn't want to start something I couldn't finish. 'Nothing,' I mumbled, feeling irritated at myself for giving in so easily.

15

Mrs Bulinski told us during registration she wanted to see the football team at break.

'I bet you anything she's cancelling training on Wednesday,' Curtis whispered. 'She'll have a meeting or something.'

I felt my heart sink but Mrs Bulinski seemed too pleased with herself for that. She had a huge grin on her face when she addressed us. 'Well, you'll never guess what I've done?' she said, dipping a chocolate bourbon into her coffee cup.

'Signed up for Arsenal?' Troy suggested.

Mrs B continued smoothly. 'Be sensible, Troy. How can I play for Arsenal and run a school at the same time? I'd never get my marking done, would I? No, this is a bit more realistic.'

'What? Tell us, miss,' Shelby asked.

'I have got you a match next week!'

A match? Much as I wanted to play against another team I knew we were nowhere near ready.

'Who against, miss?' Curtis asked.

'Tuxton,' she said blithely.

'But they'll slaughter us!' Curtis protested.

Mrs Bulinski shook her head. 'No they won't. You see, I bumped into Mr Girton last Friday at a headteachers' meeting and told him all about you and how we're just starting out and he's arranged to have his 'C' team play you. Seven-a-side after school next Wednesday. They'll come here.'

A 'C' team? How did a school not much bigger than ours manage to get a 'C' team?

'Well,' she said, looking a bit crestfallen by our silence, 'aren't you pleased? Curtis? Danny? It's what you wanted, isn't it?'

'I guess so but . . .'

'Good!' she said. 'I'll let you go and tell Mr Spanner, then.'

16

I managed to persuade Mr Spanner to let us practise on the field at lunchtimes leading up to the fixture. He agreed but turned up to 'tend' his plots like I knew he would. Everybody moaned when they saw him but secretly I was glad. We played better with the names of vegetables ringing in our ears. If only Mr Spanner showed as much interest in football as he did potatoes, we'd have been sorted but he told me he was a cricket man himself and that football was blown all out of proportion these days. Ah well.

I woke up on Wednesday morning with that familiar match-day tingle in my stomach. Sometimes it became so bad before a game, I thought I might throw up but today was just a tingle.

'Make sure you have a big lunch,' Mum advised.

Steve said he'd try and get there, Karla lent me her lucky coin, and Gran sent me a quick e-mail.

> Go get 'em, Danny.
> Let me know what happens.
>
> PS: Green's injured—hamstring.

I arrived earlier than usual at school to ask Mrs Bulinski to put a team list on the notice board. She seemed distracted and pointed to a heap of papers on her desk. 'I've got to sort out these job applications this morning, Danny, can't you do it?'

OK, I admit when I'd started all this the idea of being captain was appealing but this was managerial stuff. 'It's easier if you do,' I replied, knowing what Troy and Spencer would say if I selected the team I wanted. Unfortunately, I hadn't caught Mrs B at a good time.

'Go on, Danny. You're the experienced one,'

she said with just the tiniest hint of irritation in her voice.

But I wasn't the experienced one! Give a kid a break, missus. I tried again. 'If I write the names down will you copy it out?'

There was a curt nod of the head which I took as a 'yes'. Quickly, I scribbled down my list.

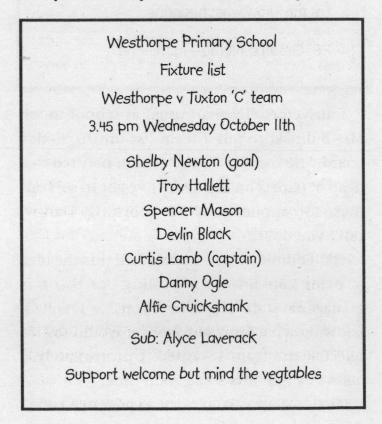

Westhorpe Primary School

Fixture list

Westhorpe v Tuxton 'C' team

3.45 pm Wednesday October 11th

Shelby Newton (goal)

Troy Hallett

Spencer Mason

Devlin Black

Curtis Lamb (captain)

Danny Ogle

Alfie Cruickshank

Sub: Alyce Laverack

Support welcome but mind the vegtables

Guess what happened? My scribbled list appeared in all its glory on the notice board with a pencil line through 'vegetables' because I'd spelt it wrong. 'I just haven't had time to copy it out,' Mrs Bulinski said with a hint of irritation in her voice that wasn't quite so tiny this time.

At lunch, more crossings out had appeared. This time, someone had scribbled out 'goal' next to Shelby's name and put it next to Troy's and somehow Spencer was now the captain.

'What are you going to do about it?' Curtis asked.

What was *I* going to do about it? After the episode at dinner time last Monday I didn't want any more confrontations with those two doofers. 'Nothing!' I replied coolly. 'What are *you* going to do?'

'See Mrs Bulinski.'

'Good luck, mate'

And Mrs B's reply to Curtis? 'Well, does it really matter who's the captain? I'm sure you can sort it out between you.' Can you imagine the England manager doing that? No, me neither.

* * *

At three forty, we paraded on to the pitch, dressed in our feeble games kits, under the feeble leadership of Spencer flipping-feeble Mason.

We stood and watched as a new minibus pulled up at the side of the road. A tall man with a bald head and long nose like Postman Pat's emerged—presumably Mr Girton—followed by his team. They walked briskly after him in single file, all kitted out in dark green strips with yellow and green hooped socks. Very smart.

'They're a bit little, aren't they?' I asked. Hardly any of them looked more than seven or eight years old, apart from two at the back.

'That's Adam and Ellie,' Curtis cried out, waving to them, 'the Huckerby twins, remember, we told you they'd moved to do more sport.'

'They don't look very happy about it,' I said, glancing at their long faces.

'They're not. Ellie told me she hates school now.'

I shrugged. It was not my problem.

Mr Girton was refereeing, with Mrs Bulinski and Mr Spanner both watching from the touchline. Alyce and the twins stood nearby, chatting. 'Ten minutes each way,' Girton declared briskly, blowing his whistle to start.

With that sound, I forgot everything. I just wanted to play.

I intercepted their first pass from the kick-off and crossed the ball to Curtis. Curtis ran halfway up the field, swerving round a defender and crossed to Devlin who just had to tap it in. The goalie, a curly-haired kid with freckles, looked lost against our full-sized goalposts and

didn't have a clue which way to dive. One–nil in ten seconds. Dream start!

Mrs Bulinski clapped politely and Mr Spanner frowned as the lad trampled across his potatoes to retrieve the ball. The goal gave us the boost we needed and we were away. I held mid-field, feeding and assisting with Shelby alongside. Spencer stayed back in defence and Alfie just ran anywhere his little legs could carry him. By half time it was five–one to us, with Devlin scoring four and Curtis the fifth.

I should have been happy but I wasn't. It was too easy. The Tuxton team were trying but we were just older and bigger and stronger. Spencer was the worst; he just barged into anyone approaching the goal, sending them flying with his rough tackles, despite being cautioned a

couple of times by an increasingly angry Mr Girton. 'This is so easy,' he bragged, exchanging a hi-five with Troy at half time.

Mr Girton obviously thought so too. He subbed his two defenders for Adam and Ellie, muttering furiously into each twin's ear as he did so.

'I might as well use our sub, too,' Spencer said and indicated for Alyce to get ready. 'You're off, Ogle,' he shouted.

Big surprise.

Strange as it sounds, I wasn't that bothered. This match was turning into a joke as far as I was concerned.

It looked worse from the touchline. Even with the twins, Tuxton couldn't make much impact on the game. Devlin was just in a class of his own. Part of me willed him to have the ball all the time so that I could enjoy his performance, part of me felt sorry for the opposition. I think Devlin did, too. By his eighth goal he had begun apologizing to the goalie and started fetching the ball for him. The poor kid was nearly in tears.

'We seem to be doing very well,' Mrs Bulinski whispered to me.

'Yeah,' I replied, 'just a bit.'

Girton blew the whistle a minute early. 'What do you say, team?' he barked. 'Three cheers to Westhorpe. Hip hip . . .'

Spencer, as captain, should have returned the gesture but was too busy punching the air in victory. Fortunately we had Alfie, who went up to each dejected player and shook their hand in turn before going back into school to get changed with the others. I hung around, planning to help Mr Spanner with any damaged plants—a deal's a deal.

I overheard Girton refuse Mrs Bulinski's invitation to come back into school for refreshments. 'No time, sorry,' he said, a tight smile on his lips.

'Well, thank you for coming,' Mrs Bulinski began.

'Huh! Well, you certainly had me fooled, Laura,' he snapped.

'Pardon?' she asked, her face going slightly pink at Girton's tone.

'Not played before? Just starting out? Do you think I would have turned up with that shambolic lot if I'd known you had a ringer?'

Mr Girton's face was turning a nasty red. I'd seen it before; that dark, threatening colour on faces of managers who couldn't bear losing, on parents' faces, screaming from the touchline if their kids made a mistake.

'A ringer?' Mrs Bulinski asked.

Mr Girton almost spat. 'A ringer—a pro. The lad who needs a haircut!'

'Oh, you mean Devlin.'

'Whatever his name is. Whose books is he on?'

'Er . . .' Mrs Bulinski hesitated, puzzled by the question, 'he's fond of animal stories—*Lucy Daniels* and . . .'

'Not those sort of books! Never mind. I want a return match next week. At Tuxton, on a proper seven-a-side pitch. Four o'clock sharp.'

'Well . . . of course . . . Terry . . . that'll be all right, won't it, Danny?' Mrs Bulinski asked, catching sight of me.

'I'm not sure, miss,' I began.

Girton cut me dead. 'That's fine, then, four o'clock. Twenty minutes each way.'

With that, he stormed off.

'I've never seen him like that before,' Mrs Bulinski said.

'I'll bet he's never lost eleven—three before,' I replied.

17

I had a bad feeling about next week's match which nobody seemed to take seriously.

'We'll just be more even,' Curtis said. 'It'll be a better game. Chill out, Danny.'

'You don't have to play if you don't want to, Ogle,' Spencer quipped. 'We scored more goals in the second half without you.'

I didn't let him get to me because I knew he didn't have a clue. He still hadn't cottoned on that for one person to score the goal (e.g. Devlin) another had to make the goal (e.g. me) and not just welly the ball into outer space and hope for the best (e.g. him).

Only Grandma shared my concerns. 'What do you reckon?' I asked her when I called her at the weekend. 'Hmm. Girton's not gracious in defeat by the sound of it. He'll be coming out with all guns blazing, Danny, no doubt about it.'

'What can we do?'

'Take plenty of vitamins and pray.'

I did all I could to prepare us for the return match. I hunted out some old boots and shin pads for Alfie because he hadn't any. Shelby's sister donated the same to Devlin, but he refused. 'These are fine,' he said, pointing to his well-worn trainers. They had scored eight goals last week, so who could disagree?

We practised after school a few times. Troy and Spencer didn't bother to turn up—they had better things to do than 'panic like a pudding'.

After each practice we bought sweets and pop from Mrs Dobbs' shop. The day before the match, Ellie and Adam Huckerby came in just as we were going out. Shelby told them we'd hang on for them. 'Fraternizing with the enemy,' I teased as we plonked ourselves down on the bench outside.

'They're not the enemy. Just because they go

to a different school doesn't mean I can't talk to them, does it?'

'I suppose.'

'Right then,' she said, pinching a green Skittle and grinning.

When Ellie and Adam joined us, there was only one topic of conversation. 'Are you both in the team tomorrow?' Shelby asked.

Ellie laughed. 'Us? Not likely. We've never been picked before and we won't be again. He says we're beyond help.'

'Yeah—the only reason we played against you was because he thought it would be nice for us to show Mrs Bulinski what her ex-pupils could do,' Adam sniffed.

'Well, that plan went wrong,' Alfie smirked.

'Yeah, and didn't *we* know about it the next day,' Adam said miserably.

He exchanged looks with Ellie but didn't elaborate. 'Will you be watching though?' Curtis asked.

'Oh yes—we wouldn't miss it for the world,' Ellie said. She glanced around nervously. 'You'd better warn Spencer to be careful. That was Josh Gibbons's little brother he kept cropping last week. Josh is *so* going to get even.'

'Is he good?' I asked.

'He's in Forest's under-twelve squad.'

'Oh. *That* good.'

'He's not even the best player, though,' Adam added. 'There's Max Gaskin, Simon Machin, Joachim, Hannah . . .' He reeled off a load more names. What made it worse was you could tell he wasn't even bragging about it, just stating facts. My worries about the match multiplied faster than bugs in mouldy fish.

'Well, we've got Dev,' Alfie said proudly. 'Nobody can be better than Dev.'

The twins stared at Devlin admiringly. 'You were brilliant,' Ellie said, 'but . . .'

'But what?' Shelby asked.

'But Mr Girton says one player doesn't make a team and the rest of you are a bunch of talentless, untrained no-hopers who run around like headless chickens and wouldn't know the code of conduct if it slapped you in the face.'

'No offence,' Adam added.

There was a long pause as everybody took in Mr Girton's little speech.

Devlin grunted something. 'What?' I prompted, hoping for some words of inspiration from our star.

'I saw a headless chicken once,' he said quietly.

'Did you? Was it disgusting?' Alfie asked.

Devlin nodded. 'Why do you think I don't eat meat?' he muttered.

As words of inspiration go, they weren't the best I'd heard.

18

I couldn't eat a thing the morning of the match
and it had nothing to do with Devlin's chicken.
I was almost in a trance as Mum opened the
post. 'More rubbish,' she frowned.

'What is it?' Karla asked.

'From the estate agents—they know we can't
afford houses at these prices but they send the
details anyway,' she complained, screwing up
the envelope. I went to stand by the door,
hoping she would be too distracted to nag me
about breakfast. No chance. 'You need
something in your stomach to give you energy,
Danny,' she said.

I already had something in my stomach. A
massive lead weight. 'I'm not hungry,' I
complained.

She threw me a banana and said 'sit'.

The day dragged. Literacy Hour felt like Literacy Month. Maths, lunchtime, science, and music all merged into one long pain in the neck. The lead weight in my stomach got heavier and heavier until, finally, the bell went and it was time.

Mrs Bulinski was taking half of us to Tuxton in her car, Mrs Newton the other half in hers. I clambered in the back of Mrs Newton's car with Devlin and Alyce.

'Don't talk to us, Mum, we've got to get psyched up,' Shelby ordered from the front seat.

'Will this help, petal?' Mrs Newton replied, turning the radio higher. It was playing 'We will rock you' but it didn't help at all.

There was quite a crowd gathered as we arrived at Tuxton School. Ellie and Adam were there, plus several of the little kids from the 'C' team, as well as a stack of parents. They stared at us with a mild curiosity as we made our way towards Mrs Bulinski and the other half of our team. I guess we'd caused a bit of a stir last week and they wanted to see what we looked like.

'Well, they haven't even got a proper kit,' one of the adults whispered loudly as we passed.

'That's him—that's the good one,' I heard Ellie say to a man—maybe her dad—as Devlin went by. A murmur arose as word got round the crowd and everyone craned their necks to see him.

I felt a sudden stab of envy. Nobody had ever said that about me. I glanced at Devlin but his eyes were on the pitch and I knew the admiration had washed right over him. He was silent and edgy; all he wanted to do was get on with the game. We had that much in common, at least.

Girton came up to us and read us the riot act. 'Right, Westhorpe,' he snapped, 'as I seem to be refereeing again I just want to make a few things clear to you before we start. First off, I will not accept any back-chat, cheating, or foul play, is that clear?'

We all nodded but it was Spencer and Troy he was staring at. I saw Spencer whisper something to Troy out of the side of his mouth. 'Second,' Girton continued, 'as this is a seven-a-side match you will be playing on a correctly set-up seven-a-side pitch with appropriately sized goalmouth.' He pointed to the goalposts, which were half the size of the ones at Westhorpe and had proper nets attached. 'There will be no offside rule, of course, but free kicks and penalties will be given if necessary. As this is a friendly, you can play as many subs as you like . . .'

'We've only got one,' I said, pointing to Alyce.

'Really? What a shame,' he replied drily.

I glanced across at the pitch—there were at least twelve Tuxton kids out there. 'Can we bring the same people on and off, then, sir?' I wanted to know.

'I don't see why not,' he agreed. I think the

'sir' had taken him by surprise. He seemed to thaw a bit. 'You the captain?'

'No, I am,' Spencer said, barging forward. Mr Girton looked unimpressed. 'Better get your team into position then.'

'Never thought of that,' Spencer muttered but luckily Girton didn't hear.

'It should be easier to score with those smaller goals, shouldn't it?' Alfie asked as we walked on to the pitch.

'We'll know soon enough,' I said. I stared wistfully as the Tuxton lot huddled in a circle, arms round each other, doing a motivational chant. We used to do those. It really puts the willies up the other team.

'How do you want us to play?' I asked our captain, just on the off-chance he had a plan.

He looked baffled, 'What do you mean "how?" Like normal, that's how.'

We were doomed, then.

19

You know after a match on telly when managers are being interviewed and they come out with classic stuff like, 'If the ball had gone in it would have been a goal'?

Well: if Devlin hadn't been so tightly marked, we could have passed to him, then he'd have scored . . .

If Spencer hadn't been such a fouler he wouldn't have given away so many free kicks and penalties, they wouldn't have scored (so often) . . .

If Alfie had stopped standing there with his mouth open and tried to get just one tackle in . . .

If Mrs Newton hadn't put Shelby off by shouting 'Go get 'em, sweetheart!' at the top of her voice . . .

If Troy had been less of a plank . . .

Score at half time?

Seven–nil.

We had a five minute gap before the next innings.

Spencer gave us his opinion of what was wrong with the game. 'They're a right bunch of cheats,' he muttered. 'They're only winning cos it's a home match. Talk about a dodgy referee. Not one of those was a penalty–not one!'

'Yeah,' Troy agreed.

'And what's happened to you, wonder boy?' Spencer hissed as Devlin took a swig of water.

'What do you mean?' Devlin asked.

'You're playing rubbish. Get some goals in or else!'

'How can we score goals if nobody passes the ball to us?' Curtis yelled. We started arguing like mad until Alyce noticed Adam Huckerby approaching. 'Shh!' she said, 'don't let him think we're ruffled.'

We stood back and pretended we liked being thrashed. 'Nice pitch they've got, isn't it?' Shelby said, trying to keep her voice level.

'Yeah; ball's good quality too,' I added.

'And this lemon squash is jolly decent,' Alfie boomed, holding up his plastic cup against the light.

Adam wasn't fooled one bit. 'How's it feel to be losing?' he asked.

'Bog off, if you've just come to rub it in,' Troy warned.

The boy lowered his voice. 'I'm not. I've just come to wish you luck.'

'Why?'

'The good players are coming on next.'

'What?' Spencer cried.

'Oh, yeah,' Adam said, dead serious. 'That was just the B team. Josh Gibbons is warming up now—he's nicknamed you DMW.'

Spencer frowned. 'DMW? What does that mean?'

'It's the name they give to prisoners on death row in America before they're executed. It means Dead Man Walking.'

We turned in silence to where the Tuxton team stood. A tall kid with a spiky haircut looked across and met our gaze. Coolly, he

looked away, said something to another team mate and laughed.

'Right,' Spencer said, bending down and pulling out his shin pads.

'What you doing?' Troy asked.

'Subbing myself off. Alyce can take over in defence. I'm not staying on there to be done in.'

'Come on,' I said, 'you'll be all right. It's not fair to put Alyce . . .'

He came down on me like a ton of bricks. 'Shurrup, Ogle. If you think you can do any better, you take over!'

'He can and he will!' a familiar voice cut in.

I spun round in surprise. 'Gran!' I shouted. 'What are you doing here?'

'Don't you lot ever read your e-mails?' she grinned.

20

With Gran's arrival there was a buzz about the team. In that one minute of rest time remaining, she gave us all such fantastic advice we completely turned the match around. Tuxton didn't know what had hit them. Within seconds of the second half, Devlin scored. I followed up with a hat-trick . . .

Yeah, you're right. That *does* only happen in books, and stupid books at that.

We got thumped.

Well and truly thumped.

Tuxton had scored twice before Troy had had time to do his first spit. Plus they were making substitutions every few minutes, bringing on fresh legs. Not because they needed to—just to show they could.

Having Gran there did make a difference to

me, though. It gave me the courage to do some decision making. Well, *someone* had to. Just before Tuxton were about to take a throw-in, I motioned to Girton to hang fire. I made Troy swap with Shelby. Troy hesitated for a second, glancing across for instructions from his mate. Waste of time. Spencer wasn't there—he'd disappeared. Wordlessly, Troy handed over his gloves to Shelby and took up her position at the back.

Things improved a little. Shelby pulled off a few good saves and brought their success rate down from one hundred per cent to about fifty per cent on target. I won the ball in mid field a couple of times and tried to pass to Devlin but

 they still had him under wraps. 'Use Curtis! Use Curtis!' Gran shouted. I did, more and more, during our rare moments of possession. Curtis managed to get a

couple of good shots in but hit the keeper's legs both times. The narrower nets meant you needed greater accuracy.

About five minutes from time, I had possession but only Alfie was in any decent space. I lobbed the ball to him but he froze and I knew he was just going to welly it any old how off the pitch and it would be their throw-in yet again. I darted forward to receive the ball back screaming 'cabbages! cabbages!' and he stopped, grinned and played it neatly back to me.

For once, Devlin had escaped and he sprang across to my right. 'Man on!' Gran shouted, but I'd already crossed it to Dev. He dribbled between two players, dummied a third and

shot from just inside the halfway line. Bang! Straight into the back of the net.

It was the best goal of the match. Tuxton were rattled then, and Devlin scored another two in quick succession but Girton blew the whistle and it was all over.

Readers who don't want to know the final score, look away now.

(It was 13–3 to them!)

21

Gran gave me a proud hug. 'Well played,' she said.

'Er, Gran, we were hammered.'

'It's only your second match as a team, what do you expect? You did your best, that's what counts.'

'Try telling them that,' I said as we watched the rest of the team shuffle miserably towards the car park.

'Oh, they'll live,' Gran said unsympathetically, 'a good team always bounces back. I told you about that time Town lost ten–one to Man. City, didn't I?'

'Once or twice,' I said, almost managing a smile.

'And look where they ended up a couple of years ago—ha! No, Danny, there's always another match, always another season. You've got the makings of a good team there, if you cut out the rubbish.'

'Do you mean Alfie?' I asked quietly.

'What, the little lad running round in circles? No, I don't! At least he tried. I mean that little slack-jack over there!' She pointed to Spencer who was mouthing furiously to Mrs Bulinski about something. 'I can't stand that sort of bad attitude. He wants to shape up!'

'We all do,' I sighed as I walked with her to her car.

'The best thing you can do is get out there and have another match. Now give us a kiss and tell your mum I'll see her soon.'

I leaned close and kissed the side without the mole and waved goodbye.

She's ace, my Gran.

22

Mum and Steve were full of concern. 'Wow! That's more like a rugby result than a football one,' Mum said.

'No need to rub it in, Mum.'

'Never mind, Danny,' Steve smiled, 'we've got something to tell you that might cheer you up.'

'Oh, yeah?' I asked.

He slid a folder across to me. 'Your mum and I have just looked round this place. It's called Chestnut House and the good news is, it's in Tuxton.'

'Tuxton?' Karla said grumpily.

'Yes, land of the mighty footballing school!' Steve grinned.

'What about me? I like it here. I want to stay here! I've just settled!' Karla sulked, stalking off.

Mum and Steve exchanged helpless looks.

'I'll go,' Mum sighed, following Karla upstairs.

'What do you think?' Steve asked, pointing to a photograph of a semi-detached house with a huge chestnut tree in the front of it.

'I don't know,' I replied.

'It's got a superb lawned garden and it's only a five minute walk to the school,' he continued eagerly.

I stared at the photograph. The house looked fine—much better than anything we had seen so far. 'We've made an appointment to look round at the weekend,' Steve stated, 'and it's empty—we could move in straight away.'

I didn't sleep much that night. I had these two voices in my head, arguing with each other. 'Well, you have to be out of the cottage in a few weeks anyway, so siding with Karla won't do any good,' one voice said. 'And the house is in Tuxton. You could be playing alongside Josh Gibbons and all those other kids. You could have Girton as a teacher—just think of those lovely, long games lessons!'

'Yeah, but Tuxton doesn't have Curtis and Alfie and Devlin,' the other voice said. 'And

Mrs Bulinski is kind and teaches well, even if she isn't big on sport.'

'So what?' sneered the first voice. 'Football is all that matters.'

I woke up confused. What I needed was a sign.

And there it was, greeting me first thing when I arrived at school.

> **There will be no more football practices until further notice.**
>
> *Mrs Bulinski*

'What's that all about?' Curtis groaned.

'Don't ask me,' I said.

'Let's ask her.'

'We can't, she's discussing the teachers' interviews with Mummy and the other governors,' Alfie informed us.

Spencer solved the mystery. 'My dad's done that,' he smirked.

'What do you mean?' I asked.

'He phoned Mrs Bulinski up at home last night and gave her a right ear-bashing about us playing a top team when we weren't ready. My dad told her she could get sued for putting us through such a traumatic experience. I bet that's why she's stopped the practices.'

I couldn't believe what I was hearing. 'Well, that's just what we need, isn't it? Fewer practices are bound to make us better players. That makes sense!' I burst out.

'Keep your hair on,' Spencer replied coolly. 'She won't do anything, she never does.'

'Exactly! That's the whole point! It takes her all her time just to turn up and now she's not even going to that! Nobody else will do it so we're finished, aren't we? No more Westhorpe Primary School Football Team!'

Spencer just shrugged as if to say 'so what?' Trust him to ruin everything. I could feel the anger bubbling up inside me like hot fat in a chip pan. I knew this time I wouldn't back off. 'You've really messed up,' I said fiercely, wanting him to make just one crack—just one.

Then Alfie let me down. 'Maybe it's for the

best,' he sighed, 'maybe we should just go back to playing in my garden again and forget being a team. We were slightly pathetic yesterday.'

Then Curtis let me down. 'Yeah, and at least we won't have Spanner staring at us all the time at Alfie's.'

Then Alyce let me down. 'And I'd like to see Justout's famous missing tinky-winky,' she grinned.

The best bit was, they were being serious. I thought of Chestnut House, empty and waiting in Tuxton. 'Fine!' I cried, throwing my hands up in despair, 'go back to Alfie's if that's what you want but you can count me out. I want to play proper football with a proper team, not a bunch of losers who give up the first time something lousy happens to them.'

They stared at me in stunned silence. Then Spencer finally stuck his oar in. 'Tch! Listen to him! He's not even that good—all he does is run round shouting orders at people—any nerd can do that!'

That did it.

Mason was toast.

I clenched my fist, ready to punch his lights out but bloomin' Devlin held me back. I struggled but he had a strong grip. 'He's not worth it, Dan,' he hissed in my ear, 'his type never are. They start it but you're the one who gets done, especially when you're new. Let it go.'

'Gerroff, Devlin!' I yelled, still too angry to listen to common sense.

'Devlin's right,' Troy added. *Troy* added?

I blinked at the older kid. 'What?'

Troy stared calmly back. 'He's right. Spencer's not worth it.'

'What are you trying to say?' Spencer asked his mate, a confused look on his face.

His mate squared up to him. 'At least Danny

stayed on the field yesterday. He's got more guts than you have!'

'How has he?' Spencer blustered.

Hallett glared fiercely back. 'You dropped us all in it, Spenny. Whatever happens you don't let your school down like that. My dad killed himself laughing when I told him the score but he got mad when I told him what you'd done. He said that was yellow. You weren't Dead Man Walking yesterday—you were Dead Man Poohing!'

'Say that again,' Spencer snarled.

Troy repeated the accusation, spacing the words out deliberately slowly. 'Dead Man Poohing!'

'That does it, maggot breath!' Spencer screamed and let fly.

It was a great scrap.

Pity Mrs Speed stopped it halfway through.

* * *

'Blimey,' Curtis said, scratching the back of his neck, 'I've never seen them fall out before.'

'Did you see that punch? Troy ought to take up boxing!' Shelby added.

Alfie was still gazing after the troublemakers. 'I hadn't thought of it like that before,' he said, frowning.

'What?' I asked.

'What Mr Hallett said about letting the school down. We did a bit, didn't we?'

I shrugged, 'They were a stronger side—we were always going to lose.'

'I suppose,' Alfie agreed, 'but we didn't need to lose so heavily, did we? If we'd listened to you more about drills and things.'

Finally!

'Yeah, and they already knew about Devlin —other teams don't,' Shelby continued excitedly, 'which means we stand a better chance next time we play a game.'

'Yes, oh yes, of course! Because if Tuxton are the best, other teams aren't the best!' Alfie cried.

Curtis turned to me. 'You didn't mean it, did you, about playing for another side, Danny? You're one of us, right?'

I looked at the ground and didn't answer.

We were all called in to Mrs Bulinski's office to give our side of the story. I'd never seen Mrs Bulinski so cross. Jets of spit flew out of her mouth as she rounded on us during our explanation. 'This just sums up that silly game totally as far as I'm concerned!' she bellowed, glowering furiously at Spencer and Troy who were standing, heads down, next to the photocopier. 'Fighting! Over football! Of all the idiotic things!'

She paced up and down a few times before scribbling her signature at the foot of a letter. I glanced briefly at it , saw it was for Mr and Mrs Hallett, then waited until she slotted the letter into an envelope. 'Aren't there going to be *any* more practices after school, miss?' I asked nervously. She didn't know just how important her answer was.

Mrs Bulinski glanced coldly at me. 'Can you give me one good reason why there should be, Danny? Because I can't think of one. In the space of two weeks I've been accused of . . . of match-fixing, I've been accused of destroying a child's self-esteem . . .' Her eyes drilled such a hole in to Spencer's back I thought he'd split in half. I opened my mouth to speak but she'd really got ants in her pants. 'And now this! Fighting—and in front of the governors—as if I hadn't enough on my plate with interviews tomorrow. Competitive games just bring out the worst in people and this just proves it,' she fired. I opened my mouth to protest but the woman wasn't even stopping for breath. 'I've always felt so,' she railed. 'Oh, it's fine for those few who have talent but what about those who haven't? Those who are picked last every time there's a Games lesson because nobody wants them on their team? Being made to feel like a reject because you're too fat or too slow or too clumsy? It doesn't count that you're good at playing the clarinet or have the singing voice of an angel. Oh no, it's how well you can kick a ball that counts in this day and age. Well, not in my school it isn't! I always vowed no pupil of mine would go through what I had to—'

She stopped abruptly and blinked, then added limply, 'Anyway, I miss Gardening Club.'

25

It didn't take a genius to work out who the slow, fat, clumsy kid was. It was crystal clear now why Mrs Bulinski hated Games. Still, did it matter? By Christmas I could be one of Girton's lads, playing all the soccer I'd dreamed of, wearing a smart kit, practising with proper equipment—the lot. I had wanted a sign and here it was but . . . but deep down, it wasn't the one I wanted. I glanced round the room.

Apart from Troy and Spencer, I liked everyone here, even Mrs B, if she'd calm down a bit. And I mean really liked—like best mates standard liked. OK, Spencer and Troy were pains in the butt at times but there had been bigger pains with bigger butts at my old school, too. And who was to say Tuxton kids would be any better—in fact, *could* they be any better? Who could make me laugh more than Alfie or impress me more than Devlin? They thought of me as one of them—Curtis had just said so, hadn't he? I couldn't let them down. I made my decision there and then. I'd play football like I supported football—not for the glory team but for the team where my heart was. I would stay at Westhorpe. All I had to do now was convince Mrs B to change her mind about practices.

'Miss,' I said quietly, 'I know what you must think about football but you're only getting one side of the picture. It's like whenever there's any trouble at an international, the cameras only show the idiots having street fights.'

'Letting their country down!' she exclaimed bitterly.

'But it's only a few that mess it up for the rest of us. The cameras never show you the thousands of normal fans just singing and cheering their team on. In fact, if you came to where I sit in the Town ground, you'd think you were in a library, it's that quiet sometimes.'

She gave me a brief, polite smile but then glanced at her watch so I hurried on desperately.

I thought of all the PSE lessons and assemblies she loved taking. 'And playing football here has helped me to settle in to school. I've made new friends quickly and that's important. My mum thinks so too; she says she'd recommend the school to anyone.' I was rewarded with a nod. 'And football's good for equal opportunities,' I said, 'it doesn't matter what colour you are or whether you're a girl or a boy or rich or poor . . .' A double nod. I was definitely on the right track now. 'Football helps family life, too,' I garbled. 'When Dad phones up from Germany, the first thing we talk about is how Town are doing. If we didn't have that we'd have those dead long pauses because we've nothing else to say—I haven't even seen him since Grandad's funeral when I was seven.'

I stopped to swallow. I never talked about my dad in front of people. Still, it was out now so I might as well carry on with the personal stuff. 'And when Grandad died, it brought me much closer to my gran. We kind of lost touch when Mum and Dad divorced and Mum started going out with Steve, especially with Dad being so far away in Germany. He's Gran's son, you see, my dad.' I thought I'd better add that bit in case she was getting confused. Everybody else seemed to be, judging by the looks  on their faces. I carried on regardless. 'We all met up again at Grandad's funeral. Gran gave me Grandad's Town bobble hat and scarf and said it seemed a shame to waste the old goat's season ticket too, so I started going with her to matches and we got back to being a family again.'

Everybody in the office let out a quiet 'ahh'. 'Gran says without football she'd be a lonely old lady mumbling to herself in the bus station,' I ended sorrowfully.

That last bit was a right fib but I could have sworn I saw a tear in Mrs Bulinski's eye and I thought I'd won her over but we were interrupted by the phone ringing. The moment was lost and we were shooed out.

26

I felt really dumb as we trooped back to Mrs Speed's lesson but Shelby gave me a friendly punch and Alfie said it was the best speech he had ever heard in his life. It was Spencer who surprised me the most, though. At lunch-time break Mrs Howells asked me to fetch the milk for the infants. As I dashed round the back of the school I almost tripped over his foot. I had forgotten he had to stand outside this entrance, Troy at the other, as part of their punishment for fighting.

'Sorry,' he muttered as he pulled his foot back.

I made for the door but Mason put his hand out and grabbed my sweatshirt. I swung round, ready to deck him if he started, but he let go instantly. 'I thought it was good—all that stuff you said to Mrs Bulinski,' he said. He sounded serious enough.

'Yeah, well . . .'

'I'm gonna get my dad to phone her, you know, and tell her he didn't mean it about suing.'

I was tempted to say something like: *'Pity he said it in the first place, dingbat,'* but something about his manner stopped me. He reminded me of that football I'd found in the shed that day—battered and deflated.

Mason kicked a small pebble across the tarmacked path, looked briefly at me then away again. 'He's like me is my dad . . . he gets mad quick . . . then afterwards he wishes he hadn't said half the things he said . . .'

'Yeah, well.'

'And you know what you were saying about your gran and grandad and that?'

I nodded.

'My dad hasn't spoken to my nan for years and we're not allowed to talk to her even though she only lives on the farm across from us. I never even get a birthday card. Nothing. Don't tell anyone, though.'

'I won't.'

'And you know all that Yorkshire Pudding stuff I come out with—I don't mean it, it's just a joke.'

'Jokes are meant to make you laugh,' I said.

'Yeah,' he agreed sorrowfully, 'I know, I'll ease off.'

Blinking heck—he'd be hugging me in a minute! I tried to think of something friendly in return. 'Your eye looks swell,' I laughed.

Gingerly, Spencer touched the puffy eyelid. 'Troy always could thump hard,' he said, flinching slightly.

'Mates, eh?' I mumbled. There was a pause. I remembered the milk and began to walk off but Mason held me back again, less roughly

this time. 'It's been good since you came,' he said unexpectedly.

'What do you mean?'

'Getting the team going. We all wanted to play football but we could never be bothered to push for it. Since you came we've had matches and everything. You've done great. And telling her everything just then . . . that takes guts.'

I stared at him, waiting for the punchline but instead he just glanced away, looking uncomfortable. 'I'll never let the team down again, I promise,' he said.

I waited for a second but couldn't hear or see any sign of a thunderbolt zapping towards him so maybe he meant it.

That night, I informed Steve and Mum I wanted to stay in Westhorpe, even if Mrs Bulinski refused to run practices. They looked dumbstruck. 'But what about playing decent football?' Mum asked.

'What can I say? I like a challenge,' I replied.

She sighed hard. 'Talk about unpredictable.'

27

Of course, I was Karla's favourite brother again. 'Cool! We can live here now and I can have my bedroom decorated properly. I'm having purple walls, stars and stripes curtains, and one of those cabin beds that you climb up with a ladder and come down by slide and you're not going on it.'

'Yeah, right,' I said, 'and I'm having mine done out in blue and I want a hammock all the way across the ceiling but there's just one small problem—this isn't our house. We've got to leave at the end of December remember, when the owners come back from Dubai.'

She shook her head vigorously. 'They're not coming back! The man's got to stay another two years so he says he might as well sell the cottage and we can buy it.'

'Since when?'

'Since last week but Mum and Steve didn't want to say anything because they were trying to find you somewhere else because of your stupid football! Favourite!'

'As if!'

'As if not!'

'I can prove I'm not their favourite,' I said.

'How?'

'Like this!' I picked up one of the cushions from the back of the sofa and belted her over the head with it.

She let out a massive roar and swiftly took up her weapon, the other cushion, and lunged. The battle had begun. It didn't take long for Mum to come charging in. 'Now what?' she

blared, calming down when she saw we were only messing about.

'We're just doing our homework!' I lied unconvincingly.

'What is it? Drama?' Mum fired.

'No, we've got to think of three questions to ask the new teachers,' Karla said, managing to drop her cushion behind the table before picking up her notepad.

'Yeah,' I said, admiring her for her quick thinking. 'Three questions.'

'I'm being serious,' Karla laughed, showing me what she had written.

1. Are you strict?
2. What is your favourite colour?
3. What is your favourite book?

By Karla Maria Ogle aged 8

'I'm looking for a sometimes, bright orange, and *Matilda* as my perfect combination,' she informed us.

'And what are you going to ask, Danny boy?' Mum teased, hands on hips. I scribbled something quickly.

'Show me,' Karla said, snatching at the pad. She shook her head and sighed.

1. Do you like football?
2. What football team do you support?
3. Will you be willing to train our football team after school?

Danny O.

'You are so sad,' she said.

After supper the four of us had a long chat about how things had changed since we'd moved to the countryside. Steve said he had a lot more work because there wasn't as much competition as in the towns. He'd already got bookings for weddings all through the following summer. Mum said she felt less stressed knowing she didn't have to worry about us getting squashed by a juggernaut every time we went out on our bikes. Karla said she liked walking to school on her own instead of having to go in the car.

'What about you, Danny?' Mum prompted. 'What has been the biggest change for you?'

'Apart from going to a new school, making loads of new friends, being an hour and a half away from the Town ground instead of ten minutes, and playing football for a side who went down thirteen–three you mean?'

'Yes, apart from that.'

'Nothing much.'

28

Now that I was definitely staying at Westhorpe, I took the interviewing process a little more seriously. Well, I was a country boy now; these things mattered. We don't have the luxury of dozens of teachers all in one school like townies. If we get a bad one we're stuck with them right from Year Three to Year Six. Think about it!

So when Mrs Bulinski introduced us to the four candidates the next morning, I scrutinized them thoroughly.

Candidate one fell at the first hurdle as far as I was concerned. 'I don't like football, I'm afraid,' she said, 'I think it's over-rated.'

Not as over-rated as your haircut, I thought.

Candidate two wasn't much better. 'I don't mind when it's the World Cup or something but otherwise I prefer rugby.'

Rugby? They couldn't even get the ball the right shape.

Candidate three was the bloke, a Mr Pearson. 'Yes, I like football,' he said. I felt my hopes rise. On to question two. 'Which football team do you support?'

'Manchester United.'

'Why?'

'That wasn't your third question,' Karla pounced.

'Why?' I repeated. 'Are you from Manchester?'

'No, I'm from Bristol. It's just that I've always supported them.'

'Will you train our football team if you are selected today?' I asked.

'Sure, if I've got time,' he agreed.

Hm. Apart from his choice of team, the guy had possibilities.

Candidate four was a Miss Craig. Her answer to my first question? She loved football. Her answer to my second question? Mansfield Town.

'I think you should always support your local team,' she explained when asked the reason for her choice.

Her answer to my third question? 'I'd love to.' *Love to!*

Well, it was all too obvious, wasn't it? 'The job's yours!' I told Miss Craig.

She smiled. 'Does that mean I don't have to meet the governors?'

29

The good news was, Miss Craig was offered the job and accepted it; the bad news was, she couldn't start until after Christmas. 'It's only eight weeks away,' Alfie pointed out.

'That's eight weeks without training,' I pointed out back.

'No, it isn't,' Alfie said smugly, 'look.'

He stood aside to reveal a new notice.

Westhorpe Football Team
Practices will begin after
October half-term.
Wednesday lunchtimes

Mrs Bulinski

Please note: practices will be cancelled <u>immediately</u> if there is any bad behaviour.

'Bless her little pop socks!' I grinned.

Practices were totally different this time. Nobody argued. Nobody complained about drills and set plays. We all just got on with it. Even Spencer. I think the fight with Troy had knocked some sense into him because he was way less mouthy. There were no more comments about gyppos and Yorkshire Puddings from either of them. It was all 'Over here, Danny' and 'Played, Dev.'

Even Mr Spanner seemed happy to let us practise without doling out the scowls and grunts. Once, when Alfie had managed to dribble the ball halfway down the pitch without tripping up, the caretaker actually clapped and muttered something amazingly close to, 'Well done, lad.'

'You know what's happening,' I said as we trooped off after our last practice before Christmas holidays.

'What?' Curtis asked.

'We're actually playing like a team.'

There were a few nods. 'Thanks to you, Oggy,' Curtis said, clapping me hard on the back.

'Yeah,' I agreed, 'I am pretty brilliant, aren't I?'

'Big head,' Alfie laughed and cupped his hands together half-singing, half-shrieking, 'There's only one Danny Ogle, one Danny Ogle, but he is an ugly kid!'

I was about to whack him when Shelby and Alyce fell into step next to me. 'Ask him,' Alyce nudged.

'No, you ask him,' Shelby replied.

I stared at them both and walked faster. There'd been a lot of sloppy stuff going on at end of term discos and parties lately. I began to get worried. 'What?' I snapped, thinking if one of them yanked a sprig of mistletoe above me it was better to get it over and done with quick.

'Do you think we could take on Tuxton again?' Shelby asked.

''Course we could,' I replied with relief.

'We'd still lose, though, right?'

'Let's have a think,' I replied. 'We don't have a coach yet, they do, we don't have any proper equipment, they do, we don't have a decent strip, they do. The answer is—probably,' I conceded, 'but the best thing about football is that it ain't over till the referee walks off with his guide dog.'

'A straight yes or no would have done,' Shelby grumbled.

'Well, I don't know, do I? Why, anyway?'

'Just curious,' she said, wiggling her eyebrows up and down. 'Ellie told me Mr Girton's arranging a massive seven-a-side tournament in March. He's inviting all the local schools.'

'And talent scouts from Lincoln and Nottingham will be there. It's going to be a biggie,' Alyce added.

'We'll be there too!' I said instantly, 'Watch out for Westhorpe!'

Shelby grinned. 'I thought you'd say that. Oh, and Danny?'

'What?'

She leaned forward and gave me a right smacker on the cheek. She didn't have any mistletoe, either. They've got a nerve, these village girls.

30

I'm almost ready for Christmas. Gran's booked tickets for the home match on Boxing Day, so that's the basics sorted. I've helped trim the house and put the tree up but I'm way behind on my Christmas cards. Writing. Ugh! That reminds me. Any old mates out there who want to get in touch can contact me at:

> Danny Ogle
> Cool Cottage
> Nice Country Lane
> Loads to Do
> The Pleasant Countryside
> England

Life's great, isn't it?

The Worst Team in The World

Alan MacDonald

Illustrated by John Eastwood

1
Don't panic!

Reject Rovers were losing. Nothing new in that, but now they were on the attack. It always made their forwards nervous, especially Kevin 'Panic' Taylor.

By pure luck the ball had landed at his feet and he was wondering what to do with it. Kevin was just outside the penalty area and had a clear run on goal.

Coxley Colts' goalkeeper got hopefully to his feet. He'd been sitting down, bored to death for the last fifty minutes, without a single shot to save.

He came off his line and crouched ready to fling himself at Kevin's shot – if it ever came.

'Steady. No need to panic. Keep calm,' Kevin told himself.

He could see the back of the net and imagined the way it would quiver when the ball went in. If only he could just keep cool and for once – just for once – score a goal for Rovers.

'Shoot, Kevin! Shoot!' shouted Mr Turnbull from the touchline.

'Pass, Kevin!' yelled Persil.

Kevin looked up. He would have liked to pass. Someone else could gladly have the job of shooting. But as usual Persil was hovering way out by the corner flag.

He never came near the penalty area in case he got his kit dirty. It was all down to Kevin.

He could hear Colts' defenders pounding back to tackle him. Any second now a leg would lunge out and scoop the ball away to safety. The chance would be gone. It was now or never.

Kevin glanced up at the goal to take aim. And that was when the familiar panic set in. The goal seemed to shrink to Subbuteo size and the crouching goalkeeper grew hands like shovels.

Kevin felt hot and dizzy. He was sweating. When he swung his right leg back it felt like it was set in concrete. His toe connected with something hard ... it was the ground and Kevin fell flat on his face. The ball trundled harmlessly into the goalkeeper's gloves. (Kevin saw the disappointment on his face.)

'That's why they call you Thunderbolt, Captain!' called Persil from the wing.

Kevin didn't bother to answer. At least he'd got his kit dirty. In fact, his shirt and shorts were plastered in mud.

The Colts' goalkeeper kicked the ball upfield. It bounced once on the halfway line. Stringbean, Rejects' central defender, jumped to head it, but too early. His lanky body – all knees and elbows – went down as the ball was going up. It bounced over his head and one of Colts' strikers ran on to collect it.

There was only Rejects' goalkeeper, Scuba, to beat. He stayed on his line.

Scuba never came out in case someone dribbled round him and made him look stupid. He preferred to look stupid in his goal. But he always dived with great style – that's why the team called him Scuba.

The Colts' striker shot and the ball soared towards the right hand top corner.

Scuba dived spectacularly towards the bottom left hand corner. The ball bulged in the net.

The Colts' striker grinned and shook his head in disbelief. He shook hands with his team mates. There wasn't too much celebration. After all, it was his fifth goal that afternoon and the score was 11-0. The referee blew his whistle soon after.

'Bad luck, lad,' he said to Kevin, picking up the match ball. 'Someone's got to lose. You lot make it look easy.'

'Yeah,' said Kevin, 'we've had a lot of practice.'

They trudged off the pitch miserably.

'Why didn't you score? You had an open goal!' Scuba moaned to Kevin.

'The ball bobbled. The pitch was hopeless,' scowled Kevin.

'Not as hopeless as you. What use is a captain who panics every time he sees the goal?'

'What use is a goalkeeper who always dives the wrong way?' Kevin snapped back. 'We'd do better with a stuffed dummy in goal. At least it would keep still.'

'No point you two arguing,' said Mr Turnbull, Scuba's dad. 'You were just unlucky, that's all. The slope was against you in the second half.'

Kevin caught Scuba's eye and almost grinned. They knew Mr Turnbull had been reading his newspaper for most of the match.

He always said the same thing. Whether the score was 5-0 or 22-0, Rovers were always unlucky according to Mr Turnbull.

He only came because Rovers used his builder's van as their team coach.

It was a good job their kit was red; it didn't show the brick dust too badly.

'You never lost *again*, did you?' a mocking voice called behind them.

Kevin turned his head to see Sean Slack. Slack played for Eastley Dynamos who had been playing on the next pitch.

Dynamos were top of the District Junior League, as Slack never missed a chance to remind them. He was the last person Kevin wanted to talk to right now.

'Don't you want to be with your own team?' Kevin asked.

'S'all right,' said Slack. 'I just wanted to know how you got on. Out of interest.'

'I suppose you won again?' asked Scuba, avoiding the question.

'Four-one,' said Slack. 'I scored a hat-trick, if you're interested. It could have been more but I'm saving myself for our next game.'

'Why? Who are you playing?'

Even as he asked the question Kevin knew the answer.

'Don't you know? We're playing you in two weeks' time. It's going to be a massacre. I've told the ref to bring his pocket calculator to keep the score.'

Kevin let out a silent groan. Scuba closed his eyes. He was imagining picking the ball out of the net every ten seconds for an entire match.

'Anyway,' said Slack, as neither of them spoke, 'you haven't answered my question.'

'What question?' said Kevin. He was trying to run on ahead.

Slack kept up with him. 'Today. Did you lose? Again?'

'Yes.'

'What was the score then?'

'Eleven-nil,' said Kevin. 'It could have been more but we're saving ourselves for our next game.'

They'd reached the pavilion. With relief, Kevin and Scuba went inside.

But Slack followed them into the changing room. He hadn't finished rubbing it in.

'So tell me again. How many games is that you've lost in a row?'

'Get lost, Slack! We're getting changed!' said Kevin.

'But how many? Just tell me, then I'll go. Have you won any games this season?'

'No!'

'Drawn any?'

'No!'

'So you've lost *every single* game?'

'I just said so. Now get out!'

'And you lost them all last season. So how many games is that all together?'

'Why does it matter? What's it to you?'

'I just want to know.'

'Thirty-nine games, okay?'

Sean Slack whistled.

'Thirty-nine defeats in a row. Is that some sort of record? You could be the worst team in the world.'

'Get lost, Slackpants!'

Slack retreated out of the doorway in a hail of football boots and shin pads.

He made his way back to Dynamos' changing room, grinning to himself and shaking his head. 'Thirty-nine games in a row. Maybe that *is* a record. I'll have to look it up.'

2

On the record

Sean Slack found his dad's *Guinness Book of Records* on the bottom shelf of the bookcase. He wiped the dusty cover with his sleeve. It was ages since he'd looked at the book.

He looked at the world's longest beard (over five metres), the world's biggest hamburger (two and a half tonnes) and the world's busiest dentist (pulled out two million teeth).

At last he found the football section near the back. There was the list of great winning teams. Man United, Liverpool, Tottenham, Arsenal ... But Sean wasn't interested in winners.

He was looking for the most hopeless team in football history. And there, at the bottom of page 124, he found them.

'The worst run of defeats was recorded by Doddering Old Boys. In the 1951-2 and 1952-3 seasons they lost thirty-nine games in a row. Their dreadful run finally came to an end with a 0-0 draw against Hardly Athletic.'

Thirty-nine games. Sean stroked his pointed nose thoughtfully.

So Reject Rovers weren't the worst team in history – yet. Unfortunately, somebody had got there first.

But Rovers had *already* lost thirty-nine games in a row. So they were only one game away from breaking the record. And that one game was against Sean's own team, Eastley Dynamos.

A thin smile spread across Sean's weasel face. Just two more weeks and he would help Reject Rovers to enter history as *the worst team of all time*. They'd never live it down. He could just see Kevin Taylor's face when he heard. And Sean would make sure the news got around.

He hadn't forgotten what had happened three years ago. Kevin Taylor had just started Rovers when Sean had generously offered to be their captain. It had been put to the vote and they'd actually turned him down. Him! – Sean Slack – with more talent in his big toe than their whole team put together.

The insult of being rejected by a bunch of rejects still made him smart with anger. Ever since he'd been waiting to get even. Now the perfect chance had fallen into his lap.

As he put the book back on the shelf Sean's eyes fell on the local paper. It lay open at the sports page.

There was the usual round-up of the local leagues by someone called Steve Ryan.

It gave Sean an idea, an idea so brilliant he had to go out to the hall mirror and blow a big kiss to himself. Reject Rovers were about to become famous!

Kevin Taylor had no idea that fame was about to call on him. At that moment he was more worried about his poster collection.

'You can put them up in the spare bedroom,' his mum told him for the third time.

'I don't want to put them up there,' Kevin protested. 'I want them here. In *my* bedroom. They're all in the right order.'

'Kevin. What's the difference? You're just being awkward about this.'

Kevin flopped down on his bed. He knew
he was being awkward but he had a right to
be. This was his bedroom. It had always been
his bedroom. And now his mum wanted to
give it to some lodger and move him into the
spare room.

'Why can't *he* go in the spare room? I live
here. I was here first.'

'I've told you, the spare room's too small,'
said Kevin's mum. 'And I want him to have a
bit of privacy. In the top room he can get
away from you and your sister arguing all the
time.'

'We don't argue all the time!' argued
Kevin. 'We only argue when she's wrong.'

His sister Fiona was thirteen, an age when
there ought to be a ban on sisters, in Kevin's
opinion.

With alarm, Kevin saw his mum starting to
peel one of his posters off the wall.

'Don't do that!' yelled Kevin. 'You'll get
them mixed up.' His football posters were
arranged in a special order.

They started with his favourite team, Man Utd, over his bed. The teams then ran along the wall to his tenth favourite, Raith Rovers (same initials as Rejects) over the radiator.

Gloomily, Kevin started to take them down while his mum cleared out the wardrobe.

'Anyway, I still don't see why we need a lodger.'

'I've told you. We need the extra money now I'm only working part-time.'

'What if I don't like him?' said Kevin.

'He sounds a perfectly nice young man. His name's Alex. He's a student teacher at Grimley High.'

'A teacher?' groaned Kevin. 'You didn't say he was a teacher!'

'Didn't I? What's wrong with that?'

'He'll talk about tadpoles and magnets. He'll want us to line up for breakfast!'

'Don't be silly, Kevin. I bet you'll like him.'

'Oh yeah? What team does he support?'

'How do I know? He may not even like football. There are people in this universe, believe it or not, Kevin, who manage to live without football.'

'Only boring ones,' Kevin muttered. 'Didn't you ask him any questions? He could be an axe murderer. He could be planning to chop us all in pieces while we sleep.'

'As long as he washes the sheets afterwards,' said Kevin's mum, absently.

Kevin took down his last team poster (Bournemouth – he'd been there on holiday) and looked around. His room already looked bare and empty – not like his room at all.

He felt sure he was going to hate Alex. He had enough of teachers at school.

His thoughts were suddenly interrupted by the phone ringing. Thumping downstairs, Kevin picked up the receiver. A voice said: 'Hello, does Mr Taylor live there?'

'You want my mum. She's upstairs,' said Kevin.

'No I don't. It's a Mr Kevin Taylor I want to speak to.'

Kevin hesitated. He tried to think what he'd done wrong recently. What trouble could he be in? It didn't sound like his headteacher, Mr Rees, whose voice could shatter windows. This voice was smooth and friendly.

'That's me. I'm Kevin Taylor,' he answered at last.

'Oh! It's just you sounded rather young. I was told you manage a football team called Rocket Rovers.'

'Reject Rovers,' corrected Kevin. 'I'm player manager. And captain too.'

'Right. Well my name's Steve Ryan. I'm a sports reporter with *The Grimley Gazette*. I was wondering if we could come and do a report on your team.'

Kevin was stunned. Speechless.

'Hello? Are you still there?' asked Ryan.

'Yes ... yes ... yes, of course,' Kevin stammered.

'You mean "yes" we can do the report?'

'Yes,' said Kevin. He was sounding like a recorded message.

'Great! I'd like to get the whole team together. Take some pics. Are you training or anything this evening?'

'Oh yes,' Kevin lied, 'we train every evening over at Riverside Park.'

'Great. I'll meet you there in about an hour.'

Kevin put the phone down in shock. How had *The Grimley Gazette* got to know about Reject Rovers? And why on earth were they interested in a team as hopeless as them? Kevin couldn't imagine.

Picking up the phone again he dialled Scuba's number. Wait till the rest of the team heard about this. They were going to get their pictures in the paper – just like Man Utd!

3

Facing the press

All the Rovers team were at the park by the time Kevin got there. In fact, most of them had been waiting half an hour.

'Where's the reporter?' asked Scuba anxiously.

'He said he'd meet us here. What are those for?' Kevin pointed to Scuba's dark glasses.

'I thought they'd look cool. You know, for the pictures.'

'You're supposed to be our goalkeeper – not a film star,' grumbled Kevin. He sniffed the air. 'And what's that awful smell? Like cat's pee.'

'It's Persil. He's wearing his dad's aftershave.'

Kevin was about to make a speech about acting like a serious football team when a red car drew up. Out got Steve Ryan and the photographer from *The Grimley Gazette*.

Ryan turned out to be a spotty young man in a brown suit much too large for him. He strode towards them briskly with his hand outstretched.

'Steve Ryan. *Grimley Gazette*. Which one of you is Kevin?'

'I am,' said Kevin, stepping forward to shake his hand. He felt important talking to a real reporter.

'Great, Kev. This is Ted. He's going to be taking the pics.'

Ted winked and showed them a large camera.

'Okay, lads?' he said. They all nodded eagerly.

'Do you want to take the photos now?' asked Scuba, adjusting his dark glasses. 'I could go in goal and dive around a bit.'

Ryan shook his head. 'We'll do that later. First I'd like to ask Kev a few questions about the team. Shall we sit down somewhere?'

Kevin followed Ryan over to a park bench. The rest of the Rovers team went too. They had never seen a reporter and they were anxious not to miss anything.

It ended up with twelve of them squashed onto one bench.

It took several minutes for Kevin to get them all off. At last they were ready to start the interview.

'Now,' said Steve Ryan, getting out his notebook. 'Reject Rovers. That's a pretty unusual name for a football team. Why did you choose it?'

'It was kind of a joke to start with,' began Kevin. 'None of us had a team to play for so me, Scuba and Stringbean, we thought...'

'Scuba and Stringbean?' Ryan's pencil had stopped scribbling.

'Yeah, they're nicknames. We've all got them. It's sort of a club rule.' He pointed out the members of the team. 'Persil, VJ, Dangerous, Baby Joe ...'

'Baby Joe?'

'Because he can't stop dribbling ... Do you want to write them all down?' asked Kevin.

'Er, maybe later. You were saying how you got the name Rejects ...'

'Oh yes. Me, Scuba and Stringbean decided to start our own team. And we called ourselves Reject Rovers because ... well, no other teams wanted us.'

''Cos we're all useless,' put in Stringbean, helpfully. Kevin glared at him to shut up.

'And how long exactly have Rovers been together?' asked Ryan.

'This is our third season. We're still improving. The best is yet to come,' said Kevin. He'd heard a manager say that once on TV and thought it sounded good.

'But what about results, Kev? Rovers haven't won too many games this season, have they?'

'We've had a lot of bad luck,' admitted Kevin.

'Dodgy referees,' said Scuba.

'And Kevin keeps missing the goal!' added Stringbean.

Kevin shot him another withering look. He was hoping Steve Ryan didn't want to ask too many questions about Rovers' dismal record. But that was exactly the kind of detail he seemed interested in.

Kevin knew the figures for this season off by heart. *Played 19, Won 0, Drawn 0, Lost 19, Goals for: 3, Goals against: 104.*

'So if you lost all twenty games last season and nineteen this season, that means you've lost thirty-nine games in a row, Kev. That's right isn't it, thirty-nine?'

Kevin had to admit it was, though he wished Ryan would stop repeating it.

'You don't have to put that in the report, do you?' he asked. 'We don't want people to think ... you know, we're useless.'

'No, no, of course not!' Ryan fingered a spot on his chin. 'This is just background stuff, Kev. Reporters have to check out all these little facts, you know.'

After that Ted wanted to take some pictures. He suggested they just do their normal training session while he snapped a few shots.

Rovers looked blankly at their manager. *Training sessions?* They never had training sessions, only the occasional kickabout.

Kevin thought quickly. 'Line up,' he said. 'We'll start with penalty practice.'

There was a lot of pushing and shoving to be at the front of the queue. Everyone wanted their picture in the paper.

Stringbean got there first. He played for a junior basketball team and was a head taller than the rest.

He took a long run-up, almost to the halfway line, and charged at the ball like an express train.

His shot sailed into orbit about thirty metres over the crossbar. Even Scuba didn't bother to dive.

Ted's camera went click. 'Nice try,' he said and gave them another wink.

Persil was next. No one had ever actually asked him to shoot before. He took a few steps forward and scuffed the ball gently along the ground. It didn't even reach the goal.

Then it was Kevin's turn. He was beginning to wonder if taking pictures was such a good idea after all. But it was up to him, as player manager, to show that Rovers were not a joke team.

He placed the ball carefully on the spot. Ted moved in a step closer to get a good shot of him. Scuba crouched low, ready to dive. Kevin began his run up. At the last minute he looked up at the goal. That was his big mistake. Panic took over. What if he missed? What if he made an idiot of himself?

Gripped by fear, he completely forgot to
look down at the ball. His foot swung wildly
and he spun round like a top. When he
looked again the ball was exactly where it
had been before.

'Did you get that one, Ted?' grinned Steve
Ryan.

Ted winked back. 'Great stuff,' he said. 'Now just a few of the goalkeeper. Why don't you give him a few shots, Steve?'

Steve Ryan lined up his first shot. Scuba could hardly see the ball through his dark glasses.

The first shot hit him on the nose and sent the glasses spinning into the air.

The second shot hit the post and cannoned off the back of his head into the net.

Scuba let in seven out of seven. Ted took lots of pictures.

Last of all, they lined up for a team photo. Ted organized them in two rows, arms folded, just like Man Utd.

'Well thanks a lot, lads,' said Steve Ryan. 'I think we've got what we wanted.'

'Will we be in the paper tomorrow?' asked Kevin.

'We'll try and make the late edition. Anyway, good luck with the next game, lads. You'll need it I reckon.'

'Yeah, we haven't a hope,' said Kevin. 'Not against Eastley Dynamos. They're top of the league.'

'And that Sean's a useful striker I'm told.'

'Sean Slack?'

'That's the one. Twenty-one goals this season.'

'Who told you that?'

'Oh, one of you must have mentioned it. Ready for the off then, Ted?'

Ryan and Ted thanked them and said goodbye.

Kevin thought about it afterwards. He couldn't remember anyone talking about Sean Slack.

4

The fame game

Kevin had told everyone at school that
Rovers were going to be in *The Grimley
Gazette*. He hadn't meant to, he just couldn't
help it. Miles Elliot had been showing off in
the playground.

Miles was one of Sean Slack's gang. He
played for Eastley Dynamos and Kevin
couldn't stand him. Miles boasted that his
uncle had been on the radio talking about
bird-watching or something.

Kevin had waited until Miles had finished
boasting. Then he'd dropped his bombshell.

'Matter of fact, I was just talking to Steve
Ryan last night.'

346

'Who is Steve Ryan?' asked Miles, rolling his eyes.

'Don't you know who Steve Ryan is, Miles? I thought you knew something about football. Steve Ryan writes the sports page for *The Grimley Gazette*. He phoned me up last night.'

Kevin could tell no one believed him. But luckily Scuba was there to back him up. Soon they were telling the whole story. By lunchtime it was all round the school.

Kevin Taylor had been interviewed for the paper. Reject Rovers were going to be in *The Grimley Gazette*. There would be pictures. Kevin had been driven home in a silver Rolls Royce. (He'd got a bit carried away with the story.)

As the day went on, Kevin's fame grew and grew. He noticed younger kids at school whispering and pointing. When he was lining up for dinner, a first year tugged at his sleeve. The small boy pushed a pencil and a piece of paper at Kevin.

'What's this for?'

'Autograph,' said the boy.

'What?'

'You're the boy that's gonna be in the papers?'

'Yeah, that's me.'

'Well, can I have your autograph? I collect them.'

Kevin had signed his name, laughing, but it felt good. At last he was somebody at school. Everyone knew his name. He began to imagine what his photo would look like in the paper.

'Kevin Taylor, manager.' Or 'Kevin Taylor, player manager of Rovers.' Better still, 'Kevin Taylor, Rovers' ace striker.'

* * *

It was Sean Slack who first got hold of *The Grimley Gazette*. He'd run all the way to the paper shop straight after school. Kevin was coming out of the school gates. A crowd of admirers were with him.

'Have you seen it?' said Slack, running up out of breath.

'Seen what?'

'The paper.' He waved it under Kevin's face.

'Is it in there?' asked Kevin eagerly.

'Oh yes, it's in there all right. A big report. All over the back page.'

Kevin grabbed the paper. He wondered why Slack was looking so pleased. Turning to the back page, he found out. The headline was in big bold letters over a team photo of Rovers: **'Is This The Worst Team in History?'** The article by Steve Ryan said:

'*Next week, a local boys' team, Reject Rovers, will make football history. If they lose the match they'll have lost forty games in a row. Forty! That's a record. According to the* Guinness Book of Records *it will earn them the title of "The Worst Team of All Time". No wonder they call themselves the Rejects! I went to see them in training and I soon found out what makes Rovers so hopeless ...*'

Kevin's eyes skipped to the photos below –
the ball pinging off Scuba's nose,

Stringbean watching his shot enter a distant
galaxy, and him – Kevin 'Panic' Taylor
kicking thin air. *'Whoops! Missed again, Kevin!'*
said the caption.

Kevin lowered the paper in horror, unable
to read on. Why hadn't anyone told him?

They'd been tricked. The report made
them sound like a joke. They were about to
become famous as *The Worst Team in History*.
No wonder Steve Ryan had wanted to
meet them!

Kevin's mind raced ahead. What would the
rest of the team say when they saw this?
They were bound to blame him – their
manager. After all, he'd brought Ryan to see
them. And what about the others? His
friends, his class, everyone at school?

By tomorrow morning nearly everyone
would have seen the paper. They were bound
to. He'd told them all to buy a copy.

Miles Elliot grabbed the paper from his
hand. The others crowded round to see.

'There's Kevin!'

'Look at his face! What a moron!'

'He can't even kick the ball!'

'Good, isn't it?' said Sean Slack. 'I mean,
I think people should know just how useless
you lot are. The most useless team in history.
You could put that on your shirts.'

Kevin saw the look of cruel triumph on Slack's face. Suddenly he understood.

'It was you, wasn't it?' he said. He pushed his face into Slack's. 'You set this all up. You phoned the paper. You told Steve Ryan all about us.'

Slack tried to push him away. He backed off a few steps.

'Don't be dumb! Think I'd go to all that trouble? Just for your pathetic team?'

'So how come he knew about you?'

'Who did?'

'Steve Ryan. He knew your name.'

'So what?'

'He even knew how many goals you'd scored this season. Twenty-one.'

Slack's eyes betrayed his mistake.

'You're mad. He could have easily found that out himself.'

'Why should he? You couldn't help showing off, could you, Slackpants?'

Sean Slack looked round for support. The crowd around them had closed in. They sensed a fight. But Slack didn't want that. He wanted Kevin to look stupid.

'At least I've got something to show off about,' he taunted. 'Not like the worst team in history.'

'We're not. Not yet.'

'But you will be. When we thrash you.'

'*If* you thrash us,' said Kevin rashly.

'Oh yeah! You reckon we won't? You lot are so slow a team of snails could beat you!'

That was when Kevin made his big mistake. He should have turned around and walked away then.

He should have said something clever like,
'I'd rather play snails than a slug like you.'
But that's not what he said.

With everyone watching, he went up to
Sean Slack and held out his hand.

'Want a bet?' he demanded.

'What? Who'll win on Saturday?' said
Slack.

'Yeah. If you're so sure.'

'You're on.' Slack took his hand. 'And the
loser has to clean the other player's boots ...'

'All right,' agreed Kevin.

'... by licking the mud off,' added Slack.

'You must be joking! I'm not licking your
boots.'

'Too late,' said Slack. 'We just shook on the
bet.' He turned to the others. 'You all saw
that didn't you?'

The others nodded in agreement. Kevin
was shaking hands when Slack had spoken.
There was no way out. The bet was made.

The crowd round him was grinning. They
couldn't wait to see him eat dirt.

'Anyway, you haven't won yet. We'll see on the day,' said Kevin weakly. He walked away on his own. The others stayed behind with Sean Slack.

As he crossed to the other side of the road Slack's voice reached him. 'Hey, Taylor! I nearly forgot – give us your autograph will ya?'

5
Lose the lodger

Kevin booted a stone into the gutter. What had he done? He'd just bet that Rovers would win on Saturday. He might as well have bet that he'd be the first man on Mars. It was impossible. Hopeless.

They'd be lucky if they kept the score down to less than ten. And then what? As far as Kevin could see his whole life would be ruined. Rovers would be for ever known as the worst team in history. The team that had lost a record forty games in a row.

They'd have to split up. Who would want to play for them? They'd be a joke.

You'd only have to mention the name, Reject Rovers, and everyone would fall about laughing.

All that was bad enough. It had taken a genius to make it worse. The bet with Slack was the most stupid thing that Kevin had ever done.

He could picture the moment after the match. Eastley Dynamos would be slapping each other on the back. Rovers would be trailing off the pitch, heads down. Then Slack would step forward with a big smirk on his face. There, in front of everyone, he would remind Kevin of their bet.

He'd take off his muddy boots, hand them over and say, 'Lick them clean, Taylor. Go on!'

Kevin wondered if he could move to the North Pole before next week. Maybe it was too cold for football there.

He opened the back door and drooped into the kitchen. Someone was sitting at the table having coffee with his mum. Kevin didn't even glance at them.

'Ah, here's Kevin. How was school?' asked his mum.

'Don't ask,' said Kevin.

'Bad as that? Never mind, I've got someone I'd like you to meet. This is our new lodger, Alex.'

Kevin had completely forgotten that the lodger was arriving today. That was all he needed.

He turned to look properly at the person sitting with his mum.

It was a girl. Older than Kevin's sister but not *old* like his mum.

She had dark frizzy hair. It was tied back in a red band but lots of it seemed to be escaping. The girl held out her hand to Kevin, beaming at him.

'Hi, Kevin. I'm Alex.'

Kevin opened and shut his mouth like a goldfish. 'But you're … you're … not a man.'

'I know. Sorry about that. It's my name you see. Alex. I should have said in my letter that Alex is short for Alexandria. People often expect me to be a man.'

Kevin's mum nodded. 'I'd even had a shaving point fitted in the bathroom.' They both went into fits of giggles.

'Great,' said Kevin. 'Just great. Well that makes it a perfect day.'

He dumped his bag on the floor and stomped upstairs to his bedroom. Kevin's mum sighed. 'Sorry about that. He can be so rude sometimes. But he'll get used to you.'

* * *

Kevin lay on his bed, staring at the ceiling. It was just the final straw. He'd just had the worst day of his life at school, he'd made a stupid bet, and now the lodger turned out to be a girl. With his mum and his sister, that meant he'd be out-numbered three to one in the house.

His sister was bound to love Alex. She'd probably borrow her make-up and start to talk like her.

When Kevin wanted to watch the football on TV, Alex and his sister would want the other side – probably some mushy love story.

It wasn't fair. He didn't want a lodger in the first place. And he certainly didn't want one who was a teacher *and* a woman.

Why should he give up his bedroom to Alex?

That was it. Why should he? He'd get rid of her. He'd think of a plan to make sure she *didn't* stay in the house. The idea almost made him forget about the match.

By the time his mum called him for supper, Kevin had put stage one of his plan into operation. He'd phoned Scuba and asked him to come round later.

Kevin said little at dinner. When Alex tried to ask friendly questions, he gave her short answers. He went to Grimley Park Primary. It was an okay school. Yes, he liked football.

'Kevin is manager of his own football team, aren't you, Kevin?' his mum said, encouragingly.

'Yeah,' said Kevin. 'But you wouldn't be interested. We're useless. Really useless.'

'I don't know. Maybe I could come and watch you sometime,' suggested Alex.

Kevin gave her a dark look. He had enough trouble without her poking her nose in. She probably thought West Ham was a kind of meat.

When Scuba arrived, Kevin smuggled him quickly upstairs to his bedroom.

'Have you got them?'

'Yeah,' said Scuba. 'They're in here. But
you still haven't said what it's all about.'

'Let's see them,' said Kevin.

Scuba put the shoe box down on the bed.
The lid had a row of air holes in it. Inside
were his two brown pet mice, Salt and
Pepper. They climbed over each other and
sniffed the air.

'It's a shame they're not a bit bigger,'
said Kevin.

'Why?'

'Rats,' whispered Kevin. 'She'll hate them. We're going to put them in her bed and wait for the screams.'

'In your sister's bed?'

'No, dumbo! I told you on the phone. It's this student teacher, Alex. She's the new lodger. If she thinks we've got rats in the house, she'll leave. She'll be out of here like a shot.'

Scuba stroked Pepper's fur. He looked doubtful.

'It'll work, you'll see. I'll be able to have my old room back,' said Kevin.

'But they're not rats, they're mice,' objected Scuba. 'And what if this Alex frightens them?'

'She won't. She'll take one look and run out of the house. Grown-ups are like that about rats. They've only got to see one and they go round the bend.'

They climbed the stairs quietly to Alex's room. Scuba had Salt and Pepper hidden under his jumper, but no one saw them.

Alex was still downstairs helping Kevin's mum to wash up. Scuba hid the mice just under the duvet. They were bound to come out and explore sooner or later.

Ten minutes later they heard Alex coming upstairs. They watched her from Kevin's bedroom, hiding behind the door.

Alex went into her room and closed her door. Kevin gave a thumbs-up sign to Scuba. They waited for the screams.

Five minutes passed. Ten. Twenty. After half an hour, Scuba started to worry. Not a sound was coming from upstairs. What if the lodger had accidentally sat on Salt or Pepper? What if she'd attacked them with a shoe?

'Perhaps she hasn't seen them yet,' said Kevin. 'We'll have to go in.'

'How?' said Scuba. 'We can't walk in and say, "Excuse me, have you seen the mice we left in your bed?"'

'We'll say we saw a rat. Then we can find them while she's on a chair, hollering.'

They crept upstairs and listened at the
door. There was still no sound. Kevin banged
on the door and flung it open.

'RATS!' he shrieked. 'We saw a big ugly rat
come in here!'

Kevin stopped. Both of them stared.

Alex was sitting on her bed with Pepper
on her shoulder. Salt was playing happily
in her lap.

'It's okay. They're only mice,' she laughed. 'Aren't they great? Do they belong to you?'

Scuba was so relieved that his pets were unharmed, he completely forgot that Alex was supposed to be the enemy. Soon he was sitting on the bed, telling her all about his pets.

Kevin meanwhile was staring in amazement at his old room. Alex had already made a lot of changes. A guitar was propped in the corner. The walls were covered in posters of faraway places. Kevin's eye took in the Brazilian footballer with the ball at his feet.

Alex's blue tracksuit hung over a chair. There was a badge on the top pocket.

'What's this?' Kevin asked.

Alex looked up from playing with Scuba's mice.

'Oh, I'm very proud of that. It's my FA coaching badge.'

'FA? You mean football coaching?'

'That's it. I did it as part of my teacher training. It was great.

'I've always wanted to coach a football team. Pity they won't let me near the school team where I'm teaching.'

Scuba and Kevin looked at each other.

'You could coach us,' said Scuba.

'No, she couldn't,' Kevin said, quickly. 'We've already got a manager. Me.'

'But you don't know how to coach. We don't even have proper training sessions.'

'I'm the manager,' said Kevin. 'And we don't need any help.'

'Oh no, course we don't!' said Scuba. 'That's why we're bottom of the league. That's why we're going to get thrashed on Saturday. That's why we'll be the worst team of all time.'

'I saw today's paper,' admitted Alex. 'Will you really be breaking this record?'

Kevin nodded. 'Looks like it.'

'Unless we get a lot better,' said Scuba. 'And Alex could help us.'

'It's too late,' said Kevin. 'We've got less than two weeks left.'

Alex shrugged. 'It's your team. If you like I could watch you practise after school tomorrow. But it's up to you. You're the manager.'

'Kevin?' said Scuba.

Kevin scowled. 'I'll think about it,' he said.

Countdown to disaster

The next day at school started badly for Kevin. When he walked into the classroom he had the feeling that everyone was waiting for him. He sat down in his seat. Something was taped to the table.

His picture. The one from *The Grimley Gazette* that showed him missing the ball completely. *'Whoops! Missed again, Kevin!'*, the caption reminded him.

Kevin flushed red. He could hear sniggering all round the classroom.

He swung round furiously and saw Sean Slack and Miles Elliot, doubled up with laughter.

'You think this is funny?' Kevin said to Slack, ripping up the picture.

'Not as funny as your face right now,' hooted Slack.

'Give us your autograph, Kevin!' jeered Miles.

'Oooh, Kevin! You're so famous!' sang Amanda Ross, pretending to faint.

Kevin sat back down. He got out his book and buried his face in it. He didn't want anyone to see he'd gone red. It wasn't fair. He'd get Sean Slack for this. He'd show him somehow.

But that was only the beginning. Slack had been busy.

Everywhere he went Kevin found the *Gazette* pictures on display. There was one over his peg in the cloakroom. There was one on the mirror in the boys' toilets.

When their teacher, Mrs Lock, opened the register, there was another. It was the team photo of Reject Rovers with the headline, *'Is This The Worst Team in History?'*

Mrs Lock asked Kevin if he had put it there. She couldn't understand why the whole class burst out laughing.

Worst of all was lunchtime. In the dinner queue everyone was sniggering at Kevin. It wasn't until he sat down that he discovered the piece of paper stuck to his back. In black felt pen someone had scrawled:

As soon as he got home Kevin ran upstairs. He slammed his door shut and buried his face in his pillow. If this was what life was going to be like he didn't want to go to school. He'd have to stay in his room for ever. Later there was a knock on his bedroom door.

'Go away!'

'Kevin? It's me, Alex.'

'Go away!'

Alex poked her head round the door. 'It's about training tonight. Do you want me to come ... or not?'

Kevin came out from his pillow. He'd forgotten Alex's offer. He hadn't even talked to any of Rovers about going training.

'What's the use?' he said. 'We're useless. The most useless team in history. And I'm the most useless manager. You ask anyone at school. They're all coming to watch us lose the match. Slack's told everyone.'

Alex came in and sat down on the side of his bed. 'Who's this Slack then?'

So Kevin told her. He told her all about Sean Slack and *The Grimley Gazette*. About the pictures that had appeared all round school. And about the stupid bet he'd made.

Alex listened. She was a good listener. She didn't interrupt like most people. At the end she said, 'So, there's only one way out.'

'What?' said Kevin hopelessly. He didn't see any way out.

'You just have to win the match. Then you won't be the worst team of all time, you'll be heroes. And Sean Slack will lose the bet. He'll be the one to look stupid instead of you.'

Kevin hadn't really thought of it like that. Alex was right. But there was one big problem. 'You haven't seen us play,' said Kevin. 'We'll never beat Slack's lot in a million years. That reporter was right – we're hopeless.'

'Let me be the judge of that,' said Alex. 'Come on, get your kit on. And tell the others they're going training.'

An hour later Rovers' players were gathered
at Riverside Park. Alex came in her tracksuit.
She let Kevin introduce her to the rest of the
team.

They started with a game of five-a-side, so
that Alex could watch them play.

Kevin kicked off. He passed the ball to
Baby Joe. Baby Joe went on a long dribble
that took him past five players and back to
where he started. Persil hung out on the
wing, shouting, 'Pass! Pass!' When the ball
eventually came to him, he passed to
Stringbean. It would have been a good pass if
Stringbean had been on the same side.
Stringbean did what he always did, hoofed
the ball with all his might up the other end.

'Mine! Leave it!' shouted Scuba, coming out to catch the ball.

He collided with Dangerous who went for anything that moved. The ball bounced once and nestled in the net.

'Goal!' shouted Stringbean. 'At least we scored one.'

They all looked at Alex. Her mouth was still open. Kevin hadn't been exaggerating when he said that they were bad.

'Well, there's plenty to work on,' she said. Soon Alex had them dribbling in and out of rows of jumpers. They passed the ball in triangles with one touch. (Most of them had never received a pass from one of their own players.)

Scuba practised diving in goal. He discovered that when he kept his eyes open, he sometimes went the right way and saved a shot. They practised corners with Persil taking them. The tenth time Persil got the ball off the ground.

Kevin and Scuba jumped for it together.

The ball glanced off Kevin's head before he
had time to panic. It hit the inside of the
post and rebounded into the net.

'Goal!' said Kevin, astonished. 'I scored a
goal ... didn't I?'

'A peach,' said Alex. 'A brilliant header
from Persil's perfect cross.'

Persil glowed with pride. No one had ever
praised him before.

'Now,' said Alex. 'Let's hear you say it:
"We're Rovers. We're winners. We're the
best."'

It took a few tries. Words like 'winners'
and 'the best' were difficult to say. But after
a lot of laughter, they managed it.

In the end they were chanting it all around
the park. 'We're Rovers, we're winners, we're
the best!'

'Good,' said Alex. 'We've made a start. But
there's still a lot to work on. Back here for
training tomorrow night.'

Someone else had been watching Rovers
training.

As the voices faded away, two figures crawled out from the bushes.

'Ahh! I've got prickles in my leg,' said Miles Elliot.

'Never mind your leg, who was that in the tracksuit?' Sean Slack demanded.

'I don't know. Maybe it was Taylor's mum.'

'Don't be stupid!'

'Anyway, what are you worried about? We'll still murder them on Saturday. You saw. It took them ten corners before they got one in the goal.'

'Who said I was worried?' said Slack. 'We'd beat them if they had ten goals' start. Still … we don't want to take any chances, do we?'

'How do you mean?'

'Well, I'm not having Taylor winning our bet. So I bought something just to make sure.'

Slack brought a tin out of his pocket and showed it to Miles.

Miles read the writing on the label and grinned horribly.

'Itching powder. Does it work?'

Slack nodded. 'Agony. The strongest stuff in the shop. It makes your eyes water and you can't stop scratching.'

'Who shall we try it on first?' asked Miles.

'I think it might help their goalkeeper, don't you?'

Slack bared his pointed teeth in a smile of pure pleasure.

A nasty itch

As the match drew near Kevin got more and more nervous. It seemed everyone in Grimley knew about Rovers and their record-breaking game.

Slack had made sure that the news was all around the school. The newspaper report had done the rest. Rovers' fame had spread far and wide. Kevin even had a phone call from a local TV producer who wanted to bring a camera crew to the match.

Alex had done her best. She had them out practising after school every day.

By the end of ten training sessions there were signs they were getting better. Scuba, in particular, had started to save shots instead of diving aimlessly. And for the first time they were passing the ball to each other.

Even Baby Joe had stopped trying to beat the whole team on his own.

Still, Kevin knew it wasn't enough. If they were playing someone else they might have had a slim chance, but not Eastley Dynamos. Eastley hadn't lost a game all season. Beating Rovers would make them league champions.

What's more, Kevin had seen Sean Slack play. Even he had to admit that Slack was the deadliest striker in the school.

No, Rovers would need a miracle to avoid defeat.

Kevin couldn't even bring himself to think about the bet and the humiliation that was in store for him. He could almost taste the dirt on Slack's boots. It was going to be the worst day of his whole life.

On Saturday morning Scuba's dad drove
his builder's van into the car park. Reject
Rovers stared out of the windows in horror.

'Strike me!' said Mr Turnbull. 'Look at
these crowds. There must be a big game on
today.'

'There is, Dad,' said Scuba miserably.
'They've all come to see us lose.'

'Oh no! There's Amanda Ross from our class,' said Kevin, ducking down behind a seat. Grinning faces pressed up against the van windows.

'Gonna lose! Gonna lose! Gonna lose!' they chanted.

Rovers pushed their way through the jeering crowds to the changing rooms.

They were just unpacking their kit when there was a knock on the door. Sean Slack came in.

'What do you want, Slack? Your changing room's next door,' said Kevin.

'That's not very sporting, Taylor. I just came to wish you good luck,' Slack protested.

'You just did. Now goodbye,' said Kevin.

But Slack insisted on going round to each of the team one by one. He shook their hands and hoped they played well.

What was going on? As Kevin laced up his boots, he wondered what his enemy was up to.

'Hey, what are you doing with my gloves?'

It was Scuba who cried out.

Slack turned round. 'Nothing! Just having a look,' he said, innocently.

He handed the red goalkeeper's gloves back to Scuba. 'Nice gloves,' he said. 'I bet you're just *itching* to get in goal. Ha ha!'

Scuba looked at him as if he'd got a screw loose. Slack paused at the door. 'Well, good luck again, lads. You'll need it. Especially you, Taylor. My boots are going to get so, so muddy today.'

He put out his tongue and licked his lips.

Kevin turned his face to the wall. He felt he was going to be sick. Scuba and Alex were the only ones he'd told about the bet. But all the others had heard it from Slack anyway.

Five minutes later there was a second knock on the door. This time they all shouted, 'Get lost, Slack!'

'It's only me,' said Alex's voice. 'Are you all changed? I thought we'd have a team talk.'

Looking round the changing room, Alex could see how nervous they all were. Rovers were used to playing in front of two or three people (one of them always reading the newspaper). But today there was a big crowd waiting for them. Everyone from school had come to see them lose.

Kevin was already panicking and Scuba couldn't stop scratching himself.

Alex did her best to calm their nerves.

'Forget the crowd,' she said. 'Forget how good the other side are. All you have to think about is yourselves. Today is your chance to shock them all. Show them Rovers are a football team, not a big joke. I know you can do it. I've seen you in training. Let's hear you say it again.

'"We're Rovers. We're winners. We're the best."'

They chanted it. Loud. Three times. Then they ran out onto the pitch.

A great cheer went up. Looking round, Kevin saw there were crowds on every side of the pitch. Even his mum and sister – who hated football – had come. He saw Steve Ryan from *The Grimley Gazette*. There was the TV crew behind their goal.

Kevin tried to calm his nerves by taking practice shots at Scuba.

But Scuba was in an even worse state. He kept removing his gloves to scratch at his hands.

'What's up?' asked Kevin.

'I don't know. It's my hands. They feel like they're on fire.'

At the other end of the pitch, Sean Slack and Miles Elliot were watching.

'It's working,' laughed Miles. 'Look, he's scratching himself like a dog.'

'I'm not surprised,' said Slack. 'I gave him the whole tin. Half in each glove.' Slack paused to thump a ball into the corner of the net. 'The game's in the bag,' he said.

A minute later they were lining up for the kick-off.

This is it, thought Kevin with the ball at his feet. The crowd were hushed.

'Come on the Dynamos!' called someone.

'Come on the clodhoppers!' shouted someone else.

There were roars of laughter.

The referee blew his whistle.

Kevin passed to Persil. Persil knocked it back to Stringbean. Stringbean passed to Baby Joe out on the wing.

He beat two players, got to the line and crossed, the way Alex had showed him. Dynamos' keeper leapt and caught it, but the crowd had stopped laughing. They weren't expecting Rovers to go on the attack. They had come to see them buried under an avalanche of goals.

For the first twenty minutes Rovers held their own. They got ten players back to defend. They tackled hard. They passed the ball so that Dynamos had to work to get it back. They were playing well – apart from their goalkeeper who was behaving very oddly.

Scuba couldn't keep still. One minute his gloves were on, then they were off again. He danced around his goal as if ants were invading his shorts. Then disaster struck.

Sean Slack got the ball just outside the penalty area. He looked up and saw Scuba bending down to pick up his gloves. Slack let fly a stinging shot. It whistled over Scuba's head and into the top corner of the goal.

The crowd cheered and laughed. This was what they'd come to see – the Rejects playing like clowns.

'What are you doing?' hissed Kevin as he took the ball from Scuba.

'I can't help it,' Scuba groaned, miserably. 'My hands are itching like mad. I think it's these gloves.'

Kevin carried the ball back to kick-off.

'That's it,' Persil told him gloomily, 'we'll never get back in the game now. We're going to get slaughtered.'

The soft goal had knocked the confidence
out of Rovers. They soon lost the ball. Eastley
Dynamos won a corner. It came over in the
air and Scuba jumped to meet it. The ball
floated straight into his waiting gloves. Then
he fumbled it. Sean Slack was on hand to
boot it gleefully into the roof of the net.

2-0 to Dynamos.

Scuba wished he could dig himself a deep
hole. He imagined the goal being replayed in
slow motion on the local TV news that night.

Rovers had let in two goals in two
minutes. They were starting to look like
their old selves.

For the rest of the half they booted the ball
anywhere to clear it. Dynamos hit the post
and then the crossbar.

Rovers rode their luck and were relieved to
hear the half-time whistle.

Alex called them together in the centre
circle.

'What happened? You were playing so
well. Then you went to pieces!'

'It's Scuba,' said Kevin. 'We'd still be in the game if it wasn't for him. Now they're all over us.' The others nodded in agreement.

Scuba stood there in misery, scratching at his wrists. 'I can't help it!' he moaned. 'Look at my hands, they've gone all red! Someone's put something in my gloves.' He showed them the orange dust caked inside.

Kevin had seen something like it in a joke shop. 'It's itching powder!' he said. 'It must have been Sean Slack, the dirty cheat! He was messing with Scuba's gloves when he came into our changing room. Wait till I get him!'

Alex had to hold Kevin back.

'It's no good starting a fight,' she said. 'You'll just get yourself sent off. The only way to deal with cheats is to beat them at their own game. Go out there and get back in the match. Scuba, you can't play in goal with hands like that. You swap with Stringbean.'

'What, me? Play in goal?' Stringbean stared at Alex.

'You told me you were good at basketball.'

'Yes, but that's different.'

'You'll be fine. Just use those long arms of yours. Now the game's not over yet. You're only two goals down. Let's show Sean Slack he isn't going to get away with this.'

Kevin nodded. He glanced at Scuba who was busy turning his gloves inside out.

'What are you doing now?'

'I've got an idea. Alex is right. You've got to play cheats at their own game.'

'What are you on about, Scuba?'

'There's still plenty of powder in these gloves.' He put them on, inside out. 'I'll be back in a minute,' he said, and trotted over towards Eastley Dynamos.

Kevin shook his head. Scuba had finally flipped. He watched him go up to Sean Slack and slap him hard on the back of the neck.

'Well played, Sean. Great goal!' said Scuba.

Slack glared at him, scornfully. 'I've only just started. We're going to murder you this half!'

Scuba gave him a cheery wave. Then he went round the rest of the Dynamos team, slapping and rubbing them on the back to congratulate them.

'What was all that about?' asked Kevin, when Scuba trotted back.

'You'll see. Just giving them a hand!' Scuba took up his position in defence.

The game restarted. Dynamos went on the attack looking for more easy goals.

Slack took a pass with his back to goal.
Skilfully, he turned past Scuba and pushed
the ball between Dangerous's legs. Slack now
had the goal at his mercy. There was only
Stringbean to beat. But, just as he was about
to shoot, he clawed at the back of his neck.

'Yahhh! Oww! It stings!' Slack hopped
around as if bitten by a viper. Meanwhile,
Scuba calmly took the ball away from him.

'Tut tut! Nasty stuff, itching powder,' he
said, shaking his head.

Rovers took the ball upfield. Dynamos
tried to get it back, but now odd things were
happening all over the pitch. Eastley players
were pulling off their shirts and scratching
furiously at their backs.

The ball came to Kevin – he slipped it inside to Baby Joe. The Dynamos keeper came out, then had to pause to itch his neck. Baby Joe dribbled round him and scored; 2-1.

The crowd cheered and Rovers celebrated their first goal in fifteen games.

Scuba gave Kevin a thumbs-up with the gloves. 'Told you I'd give them a hand.'

'Come on Rovers, get a second!' shouted Alex, jumping up and down with excitement.

Eastley Dynamos had gone to pieces. The itching powder Scuba had spread around was affecting half their team. And the other half were keeping well away from Scuba.

Kevin went down the wing and passed inside to Scuba. Scuba advanced to the edge of the penalty area. Three Eastley defenders blocked his path to goal – but none of them wanted to risk a tackle. They seemed to be hypnotized by Scuba's deadly powdered gloves. While they hesitated, Scuba pushed the ball past them and tried a shot.

It scudded along the ground, hit a bump in front of the diving keeper, and bounced over him into the goal. Miraculously, Rovers were level.

As Dynamos kicked off, Kevin could see the wonder on his team-mates' faces. They thought they'd done it, that the game was over. But Kevin knew that for him, it wasn't enough. They had to win or he would still lose his bet with Slack.

The thought of licking dirt from Slack's boots in front of everyone was too much to bear. He'd rather lie down in a bathful of maggots.

There were only fifteen minutes left. Rovers needed one more goal but their old failings started to show. Kevin shot over the bar from five yards out and Persil fluffed an easy chance by waiting too long.

The effect of the itching powder was starting to wear off. Sean Slack looked dangerous at the other end. He would have scored twice if Stringbean's long arms and legs hadn't got in the way.

It was a nail-biting finish with the crowd urging both sides forward to get the winner.

Kevin chased the ball all over the pitch in desperation. As the final minutes ticked away, Rovers won a corner.

Just as they'd practised in training, Persil crossed and Kevin jumped to head it. He was going to score. Until someone shoved him in the back and he went sprawling.

'Tough luck, Taylor!' grinned Slack, standing over him. Slack's grin melted away when the referee's whistle blew. He'd seen the push and awarded Rovers a penalty.

There was one problem. No one wanted to take it. The Rovers players remembered too well their pictures in *The Grimley Gazette*. When Kevin offered them the ball they all shook their heads.

'Why don't you take it?' suggested Scuba.

'Me? Why me?' asked Kevin.

'You're the captain. It's your job.'

'But I'll panic. I'm bound to miss, I know I will.'

The referee blew his whistle again, impatiently.

'Go on. You can do it, Kevin,' said Scuba.

Kevin placed the ball on the spot. So it all came down to this. One shot. Just him and the goalkeeper. If he missed they would all blame him – Kevin 'Panic' Taylor – but not as much as he would blame himself.

He glanced up at the faces crowding behind the goal for a better view. There were his mum and sister, his classmates from school, and the TV camera zooming in on him. All waiting for him to miss.

He felt the panic rising from somewhere in his stomach. He couldn't look at the goal. It would be shrinking smaller and smaller.

He tried to concentrate on the ball. If he could just kick it in the right direction so that he didn't look totally stupid ...

Just as he was about to start his run-up, a sneering voice said, 'Whoops! Missed again, Kevin!'

Without looking, Kevin knew the voice was Slack's. He felt a rush of fury.

He ran at the ball and thumped it with all his might. It went high and to his left.

Dynamos' goalkeeper flung himself and got one hand to it. For an awful moment, Kevin thought the goalkeeper had saved it. But the power of the shot took it past his fingertips and into the net.

There was a moment of stunned silence all round the pitch. Then the noise erupted.

Kevin was buried under a pile of players jumping on top of him. Alex was hugging everyone in the crowd, people she'd never met. Sean Slack was chasing his own goalkeeper round the pitch.

When the game finally re-started, it only lasted a minute longer. The referee blew his whistle. Rovers had won. It was unbelievable.

They had beaten Eastley Dynamos. They wouldn't be claiming a place in the record books. They weren't The Worst Team in History. As Alex said afterwards, 'Even Man United would have been proud of that performance.'

Kevin was mobbed by friends from school. They all said that they knew Rovers could do it all along.

The TV people wanted an interview with him.

'Kevin, that was a shock result,' said the reporter. 'How do you explain the difference in your team today?'

'Teamwork,' said Kevin. 'Thanks to our new manager, Alex, we've been improving all the time. The best is yet to come,' he added with a grin.

'Did you always believe you could do it?'

'Of course,' said Kevin. 'In fact I had a bet on the result with someone. About a pair of boots.'

Kevin took off one of his football boots and held it up. It was caked in oozing brown mud.

'Has anyone seen Sean Slack? I've got something for him.'

Hiding in the middle of the crowd, Sean Slack gulped. He tried to wriggle his way out, keeping his head down. But Scuba was watching and grabbed him by the arm.

'Come on, Slack,' he said. 'The cameras are waiting. Now it's your turn to make history.'